2011
THE *Gunpowder* REVIEW

Vonnie Winslow Crist and Wendy Hellier Stevens, Editors
Published by Gunpowder Branch,
National League of American Pen Women
Harford County, Maryland, USA

The Gunpowder Review © 2011
ISBN 978-1-105-17659-3
Editors: Vonnie Winslow Crist & Wendy Hellier Stevens
Layout & Design: Book Mark It Promotions
Printed in USA
Published October 2011 by Gunpowder Branch, NLAPW
Cover photo: "Butterfly in Bloom" by Katie Hartlove
Back cover photos: "Sherwood Garden Tulips" by Danuta Kosk-Kosicka, "Tree Cathedral" by
        Patti Kinlock, "Puddle Jumper" by Kristen Stephens Crist, and "Maze" by Robin Bayne,
        "Jellies" by Jean Voxakis

The Gunpowder Review 2011 was made possible with the support of:
The Maryland State Government through The Maryland State Arts Council
The Harford County Government through The Harford County Cultural Advisory Board
Our boosters & patrons including:
  Book Mark It Promotions, www.book-mark-it.com
  Baltimore Science Fiction Society, www.bsfs.org
  Chezia Thompson Cager
  Rosemary Klein
  Julia Wendell

More information on *The Gunpowder Review*, Gunpowder Pen Women, and Harford County &
Maryland Arts Groups can be found at http://www.gunpowderpenwomen.wordpress.com

Dedicated to Barbara Kirchner
and the other the creative women who have blazed the trail.
We admire your art and words
and strive to carry on your tradition of excellence.

| CONTENTS | PAGE | CONTENTS | PAGE |

CONTENTS	PAGE

Morning Haiku

morning thoughts return
as a prayer adrift on air
this day is heaven

Jean E. Keenan

Wearing White

Birch boughs lean below
Their waists, wearing
White, peeling dresses
Like Grandma's apron
Strings with flakes and flour
Falling from them,
Brush me with their
Bent branches, cover
Me in their lean, leafy
Blankets as I stay
And hide
Here in the tall grass…

Maxine S. Petry-Anderson

Sweetness

Sweet taste of convenience
Buzzing of bees
Collecting pollen
Take a ride
Producing sweet nectar
A sweetness reborn
With each taste

Elizabeth Lane-Stevens

Gnome's Home
Vonnie Winslow Crist

Stalker

Dusk drives the countryside
with clippers in her pocket.
Aspen leaves like tiny kites
shiver their silver undersides.
But lilacs are the motive.
A telling scent trails the wind
as spring lifts the fingerprints
and cleans away all evidence
of clippers in dusk's pocket.

Patricia Jakovich VanAmburg

Spring View
Jean Voxakis

Seepage

On a spring day,
anniversary of bipolar crash,
like yesterday—
the fear comes back—
of being dark-hearted
on a pink-flowered day
when the air has freshness
and I should not feel gray.

I know what to do.
Find something,
seek someone,
walk,
phone,
anything,
but not home alone
on a glittering gardening day.

Seeping through the grass,
wet soil becomes a sponge.
I want to flit on top of it,
like others in their yards.

simmering along,
unhampered by seepage
escaping through my lawn.

Carolyn Cecil

Ingrained

A stump
remnant of a tree
a graying loss

in a wreath of green leaves
from shoots
on a foreground of pink heather
becomes the focus of the picture

Within the frame
I sit on the stump
filled with the moment's
joy

Lidia Kosk
translation Danuta E. Kosk-Kosicka

Wtopiona w obraz

Pień
po ściętym drzewie
zszarzała strata

w wianku zielonych liści
młodych drzewek
na tle różowych wrzosów
staje się podmiotem obrazu

Wtopiona w jego ramy
siedzę na pniu
w pełni szczęścia
chwilą

Lidia Kosk
translation Danuta E. Kosk-Kosicka

Yellow Flowers

Poets talk of love
But more often
The lack of it
Knowing only one raw square
Of earth
Where love grows
Untamed
Unbidden.
A weed with yellow flowers
Out of place
Among your roses
Casting tendrils
To encircle
You…
But the roses pass
As love and loss and
The weeds with
Their yellow flowers
And no one will recall
They ever stood there.

Joan Donati

---

*And the day came when the risk to remain
tight in a bud was more painful
than the risk it took to blossom.
~Anais Nin*

Wild Dogwood

All winter long
Bare black branches
Then one morning
Flocks of butterflies settled there
White and waxen
Signing spring

Marcia Kurland Miller

Blue-Winged Teal

Small dabbling duck,
wallow in freshwater,
mince your steps on the sticky fronds
of April,
rest your blue bill on your speckled chest
like a dignified dowager
looking down her nose.

Fashionable in your touches of sapphire
on breast and wings,
your color is more blue than
what the paint store calls teal,
something more moody than
turquoise,
more matte than satin.

Anne M. Higgins

Journal Entry

The view from my bench is how I remembered it from last spring…except things have spread…probably so have I. Today, Sunday, it's supper time as birds chirp from undisclosed tree locations. I surveyed the garden flanking my front walkway, blooms in brilliant fuchsia of various shades. The azaleas are in full bloom and the rhododendrons are just starting. The thistle robust! Drat! And the morning glory has seized the opportunity to run rampant now that I'm no longer a diligent gardener.

The sign in the garden reads *Gardener on Duty*, but it can no longer be seen by the untrained eye. I have shade from the cherry tree and, looking up, I realize it needs pruning. I duck to avoid being harpooned from its branches. My garden flag—wrapped around its pole in its hayday read *Faith, Hope, Love* under house motifs. Today, it was replaced by one that says plainly

G

WELCOME above a huge, healthy pineapple.

WELCOME. Seven easy letters that could earn triple in a scrabble game. It's a simple word, almost as powerful as LOVE. Perhaps it's a shorten form of "We'll Come." And I would like that very much.

Today, spring was marked by a perfect evening, basking in the setting sun on my bench. Journal in my lap, I'm ready to pen the moment to welcome the challenges of this chapter…where dreams co-exist with reality, and I'm in harmony quieted by my surroundings. WELCOME to my bench.

Gyleen X. Fitzgerald

Cherry Blossom Repose

Brilliant, delicate blossoms
beckon me on to duties
of the mundane yet beautiful.

I will glide slowly thru
feet delicate and
bound to service of
love and respect,

I will glide slowly thru
Kimono-clad dark silken
wisps of hair
frame my face and
cover my shame,

I will glide slowly thru
my destiny, my life loosens
the door of grace opens
I will glide slowly thru.

Lynn Banfi

Growing Up on The Patuxent by the Old Laurel Mill

Soon as April was over, we swam in the river.
We swam all summer, into September.
The dam's explosion? I remember
it was an overcast day, extra dark, maybe some
smoke from the blast hung in the air.

I was the house closest to the river.
I remember my neighbor coming up from there
after the dam blew. I was only seven,
too young to go
with the other boys down to the swimming hole.

But when I got to be ten, eleven, twelve,
we'd go play there every day.
We were about ten kids:
the Owens, Billy Stanton, "River" Poe,
and my brother,
who was a year older. We all swam nude.
Unless, of course, the girls came by; Sue Bell…
Then we'd slip on our britches.

First bend, second bend, all the way up
to High Rock, where the bigger boys,
high-school seniors, would dive.
(One boy, we heard, fractured his spine up
there.)
Brooklyn Bridge Road's gravel was hard on bare
feet.

Walking along the river bank we'd
pull up the "itch weed" and hurl it at one another.
This was one form of war. Our games, our fort,
the old stone walls at the mill race—
we'd climb 'em as balustrades.

I guess you know they went from grinding flour
to spinning cotton, to making canvas for
sails and tents in times of war, to "ramie,"

a string that pulled closed a tobacco pouch,
and then to window shades in the end.

When I got older there was swimmin' *and*
softball.
Then I took a job at the Laurel Post office,
married and raised up my kids, grandkids,
now great-grands
all come up to see me right here on the river,
with its bounty of wildlife, its deer and its fox,
its groundhogs and muskrats,
its herons and eagles.

Victoria Floor

My Mother's Garden

Every life lesson that must be learned came from my mother's garden. As a child I would spend countless hours wandering amidst the flowers, vegetable patches, and fruit trees, hoping to one day grow a garden as beautiful as my mother's. It was there that I learned to dig, till, plant, nurture, and prune. And through the time spent in this lovely oasis of blossoms and buds, I was taught everything I would need to know in life.

Here, I learned that you reap what you sow, that by nurturing and tending we are able to bring out the best in others. I learned the hard way that even the most beautiful of roses still bears the sharpest thorns. That, like people, we should never judge by outward appearance, for the sweetest looking berries are sometimes poison to the core, while the ugliest of weeds can often heal. While drinking in the shade of the apple trees, I discovered that the apple doesn't fall far from the tree, but a push in the right direction can move it a thousand miles.

I unearthed a significant lesson while planting pumpkins destined to become homemade pies. I learned that the more hard work and effort that is applied, the sweeter your reward will be. One summer after returning from camp, I found that not only had my mother's sunflowers grown high above our lilac bush, but that we too must be as sunflowers, always seeking the light even on the darkest of days. We must remain steadfast in optimism despite being bombarded with negative influences from our surroundings.

During Baltimore's drought of 1999, I found that without the rain all plant life would shrivel and die. Through this observation, I came to understand that without enduring and overcoming hardships, human beings would be unable to grow or thrive, that by weathering the storms with the same openness and acceptance that we weather sunshine we are able to grow to our full potential.

But the most important lessons I learned came from planting a sprig of oak tree with my mother when I was four years old. The knowledge of roots instilled within me the greatest education. Every living entity begins with roots, whether it is a flower, vegetable, tree, or person. Our roots determine the direction in which we grow. If planted in improper conditions, the roots produce a weak and breakable plant, much like being the product of a negative environment produces a broken spirit, while a loving home produces a strong and determined individual who has seen the ups and downs of life but is able to depend on their roots to see them through their tribulations.

Garden
Robin Bayne

Overpowering roots can strangle the tree. Weak roots beget an even weaker tree. Because of this observation, I was able to recognize that overbearing tendencies strangle relationships and apathy forms no bonds or loyalties. If a plant is cut or pulled away from its roots, neither survive. After watching my mother's marigolds deteriorate in a vase on the dining room table, I understood the possibility that without family and companionship the human spirit would wither and parish like a marigold cut from its roots to decorate a dinner table for a Sunday feast.

The mighty oak taught me most of all. Its roots splayed and grew beneath the bricks of our pathway, emerging through the cracks and crannies that were established by time and circumstances. Three separate trunks developed from the base of this noble timber. Monitoring its chrysalis proved to me that no matter what path you are on or which direction you grow, your roots will always be there to support you whenever you're trampled on and whenever life seems to pull you in several directions.

Every life lesson that must be learned came from my mother's garden. As an adult, I remember what I discovered there and hope to one day grow a garden as beautiful as my mother's.

Christina Durner

Fleshy Girls
Maxine S. Petry-Anderson

Summertime

I was born during the first week of June, at a time when the earth is turning so nice and warm and summer blooms are showing good promise. Spirits are warm as well, for the longer evenings arrive and windows in every house are opened to receive the fresh, soft breezes of the early summer season.

Everywhere gardeners are busy with well-worn tools, new gloves, and packets of seed or containers of bedding flowers. Fences of all kinds are holding up the last stems of tulips, daffodils, and iris. The impatients, pansies, marigolds, and lavender await the turning of the earth once more.

Women in sleeveless shirts and summer dresses stroll in parks with their children. The sun browns their shoulders and legs. They talk with each other and smile. They wonder at each others beautiful children.

This is the time of year that defines anticipation. There are three long months of outside activity, long nights of playtime and conversation with neighbors and friends. Children are worn out from play, and after a soapy bath and a soft towel rub down, they are ready to snuggle into their cool sheets and soft pillows. There is still enough light after the children are asleep to go back outside and enjoy a cup of coffee or a glass of wine with your spouse or the neighbors.

In our town, summer brings out the best in everyone. People seem to come alive after a long, dreary winter. Everyone feels friendly and relaxed. With the feeling of so much extra time, more is accomplished inside and out during this period of the year. Cars are washed, blankets are changed from winter to summer, rugs are removed, and screen doors put in place. Deck furniture is brought out, and flags are flown from porches. People gather on the sidewalk or driveway to catch up with each other and have easy summertime conversations. I watch my sheer curtains blow with the breeze in our bedroom and smell the clean, grass-like scents of the season. In the morning, I awaken to the sounds of cardinals, finches, and robins. In the evening, I fall asleep to crickets. I am happy that my birthday takes place in this beautiful month. I see more smiles, more beauty and more life than in any other month. I enjoy the warm evenings and the delicious smells of fresh cut grass and blooming flowers. I enjoy the lingering spring peepers that sing me to sleep.

Ah, June!

Victoria Corkran

Lake Smell

In late afternoon
in late summer,
we peel off our jeans and shirts
walk across sand
and into the lake up to our thighs,
make shallow dives and surface, inhale,
and then it happens—that wondrous smell—
the very distillation of a summer lake
that rockets up olfactory links to wash
the brain. Algae-green smell, scent
of first rain on sun-baked cement,
animal, vegetable, mineral smell
that soaks into skin, perfumes our hair,
breathes new life into our city souls.
But it only happens right at the surface,
after the day's very first dive
in late afternoon
in summer.

Margaret S. Mullins

Buck and the Lady in the Lake

It was a glorious mid-summer day, the kind of day that feels carefree and seems endless and timeless. Ann and I had left work early and decided to get together. We were delighted to jump-start the weekend. So without taking time to change into grubby clothes, we walked towards Wilde Lake, strolling along in our long skirts, dangly earrings, and summer sandals. Buck, my handsome, light-blond, six-year-old Golden Retriever walked happily on his leash. Once we got to the lake, I let him off leash because he was trained to verbal commands. He never ran off or got into the water without first getting permission.

Buck ran along sniffing trees and greeting passersby, always just behind or ahead of us. We casually strolled around the lake. Occasionally, we'd pause and sit on a bench to enjoy the ducks paddling along or a blue heron striding back and forth, head angled. And as we watched, two swans glided across the water, and a brown cormorant stood on the small island stretching his wings in the sun. Later, pleasant breezes blew as the sun began to settle in the west.

We had just turned on the path leading towards home when I reached around to leash Buck for the walk back. He wasn't there. I stopped and looked behind us. Buck wasn't there. He never wandered off, never even had to be called. This was weird. I started to walk, then run, along the path retracing my steps. I called his name, expecting to see him bounding towards me, tongue lolling. Nothing! I called again—louder!

Ann and I split up and raced to opposite sides of the lake, yelling his name and asking people if they'd seen a Golden Retriever. No one had seen him.

Suddenly, I saw Buck—he was in the

middle of Wilde Lake surrounded by dozens of ducks. The angry water fowl were splashing and quacking loudly because he was holding a duck in this mouth. A duck? Although a water retriever, he was not predatory. I could not believe my eyes. Buck had caught a duck? Oh my G-d! He's got a duck!

"No, Buck!" I yelled. "Drop that duck. No duck! Buck, come here! Get the stick!" I commanded, grabbing and tossing sticks in his direction.

He watched the sticks as they flew by but would not release the duck to retrieve them. I panicked. I had to save the duck.

But wait—something was wrong here. I stopped and took a good look at that duck. It wasn't moving. Wasn't flapping or quacking. It stayed upright in the Buck's mouth, like a toy! A toy? Then, I realized Buck wasn't going anywhere, either. He was treading water, staying in one spot.

Ann ran over, and we stood staring at the dog and the duck. Something was wrong with this picture.

"Buck, Come!" I commanded in my most authoritative voice. "Drop that duck. COME!" I ordered. He refused to release the duck, and he was still not moving through the water. He seemed to be stuck. As I wondered what Buck was he caught on, I realized it was the duck that was stuck. Then, I knew what was wrong: the duck was a decoy. It was attached to the bottom of the lake. It was not moveable. Buck was trying to retrieve a duck decoy. And determined retriever that he was, he would not release that decoy.

I could see he was getting tired. His eyes were wide, and his breathing was labored. I could hear little moaning sounds. His legs had been paddling and paddling; mud and sediment were being churned up around him. As I watched, his paddling seemed slow—he was losing energy.

I gasped. "He's going to drown out there. He'll go under before he lets go of that duck!" Tearing off my shoes, I handed Ann my house keys; whipped off some of my jewelry; climbed down the hill over rocks, tree roots, and underbrush. I stepped into the muddy silt-filled water and sank up to my ankles before I'd walked an inch. I trudged and sank, and trudged some more until the water was finally deep enough for me to stretch out and swim. My long skirt, now muddy and water-logged, floated around me like a billowing parachute, weighing me down and getting tangled around my legs. Fighting the yards of fabric, I propelled myself through the murky water out to the middle of the lake. When I reached Buck, I could see how fatigued he was. I scuttled up beside him and grabbed at the duck.

"Give me that duck, Buck," I demanded. He turned his head to the side avoiding my grab. He was not giving his prize up! "Give it to me," I urged.

"No, It's my duck," his seemed to say as he turned his head from me.

"Give me that duck, Buck," I repeated. Again, he eluded me, moaning his objections and holding his precious trophy high in the air.

"We're going to drown out here," I wailed. "Give me that DUCK!"

I was frantic now. I swam in front of Buck, risking doggie paddle paw-strikes, and with both hands, I grabbed the plastic duck clamped in his jaws. We wrestled for several moments—him whining through clenched jaws and me ordering him to drop it. Finally, I twisted the decoy sidewise, wrenching it free.

Pointing to land, I said, "Go!" But Buck kept circling me, trying to get the duck back. "Okay, you," I said, grabbing his collar. "Follow me."

We paddled towards land. Once headed in the right direction, Buck forgot about the duck decoy and swam steadily, reaching shore before me. He dragged his algae-covered body out of the water and began shaking himself off and rolling in the newly cut grass.

When I arrived at the shoreline, I was horrified to find that my wet clothing hampered my ability to get out of the water. My ankle-length skirt was so water-logged, it kept falling down around my ankles, tripping me. I was stuck at the water's edge, sinking in what seemed like quicksand. Having used most of my energy swimming and fighting with Buck over the duck, I simply could not get out of the lake water and climb up the hill.

Silt squished between my toes. My feet kept hitting hard, sharp things, sending prickles of pain through my body. I struggled for footing, grabbed for tree roots and low hanging branches. Ann tried to help but lost her footing and nearly slid into the lake.

At length, I called, "Buck, help Mommy."

He stopped rolling in the grass and rushed over to the shoreline. Carefully, he inched down to the water's edge and extended his neck towards me. I put my arms around him, and he backed up step by step, pulling me out of the water and up the hill. By now, people were crowding around. Now that I was on shore, we waved away their offers of help. Instead, we sat on a bench, with Buck lying at our feet for about 20 minutes, trying to slow our breathing and calm down.

I looked down. I was green. My all-white outfit was green. I was covered with algae, mossy stuff, and some kind of pond scum. It covered my head and hair and reached down my face in long slimy strands. I was pond-scum green from head to toe. And Buck looked like some mossy fairytale monster. Grass and pond scum stuck out in all directions. Each one of his blond doggie hairs was encased in algae, forming a tangle of green dreadlocks all over his body. Bathing him was going to be impossible. Bathing me was going to be impossible. And we stunk. We both stunk!

But having walked to the lake, we had no choice but to walk home. The shortest route to our house was along a nearby highway. Unfortunately, it was heavily trafficked. I hoped no one would recognize me. I kept my face averted as we walked. Drivers nearly crashed into the curb when they saw two soaking wet, green creatures dripping with plant life staggering along the highway—one of whom had to keep pulling her falling skirt up.
It was not until the following week that I learned just how well Columbia's rumor mill worked. I was shopping at the Giant, inspecting some broccoli, when Pat Kennedy, president of the Columbia Association, stepped over to me. Smiling, he said, "I hear you have another nickname!"

"Really," I replied, turning to smile up at him "What's my new name?"

With a grin, he answered, "You're not just Columbia's Liz Taylor anymore, you're also The Lady of the Lake."

And so I was!

Nancy Alexander

Virginia Stream
Patti Kinlock

After Too Much Summer

shiver in Fall's early nights
dress in purple flannel
delight in snow fragrance   adrift
through window's draft

sickle moon slices
bare   black branches
stubborn brown leaves
scratch each other in camaraderie

under white comforter
sleep like silent falling snow
wake with pungent aroma
percolating Autumn's mornings

savor mugs of hot latte
that warm cold hands
watch hands of maple leaves
wave yellow farewells to summer

Jean E. Keenan

Darlington Academy
Barbara Kirchner

Empiric Afternoons

Tiny, bare feet step through a rain puddle
and onto dry sidewalk;
the small child attached to the feet
looks back and puzzles over the footprints.
She returns to the puddle,
steps again onto concrete,
studies the evidence, looks up and smiles,
then returns again and again
to wet her feet, walk on the sidewalk, and
confirm her findings. Over and over she tries it,
tries it walking, tries it running,
tries it on tiptoe, walks in circles,
then on all wet fours, verifying the data,
reveling in the wonder of puddled feet.
On a sunny afternoon soon after,
she discovers shadows, dances
all the way to the park, runs
to step on her mother's head, circles
to catch the flapping flat shapes
of pigeons, grabs for the dog leash
always just ahead of her on the ground.
Pausing, she looks from shadow to object,
and back, studying each. Running again,
she tries to jump over her shadow,
laughs, walks backwards, and stops.
Turning to face the sun, she looks at the ground,
turns again, thinking hard and watching
as the grass turns dark and back to green,
testing and sorting the riddle of light
with each delighted spin.
And then, on a cloudy afternoon,
with a squall coming in over the harbor,
dry leaves spiraling, jacket billowing,
and her long, straight hair whipping her face,
she squeals, throws out her arms, and embraces
the wondrous possibilities inherent in the wind.

Margaret S. Mullins

G

Invoking Eternity

when we would conjure
rapturous beings united
in the tarantella

a cacophony arose
within the mute corridor

luminescent orbs glided past
like cottonwood seeds
in the wild winds which wafted
tender lilac blossoms and forest onions
under our tantalized nostrils and eyes

the tears welled and watered the ghost
grass grew a thousand petals of luscious
lilies lusting for bees to come
and be anointed

the spell was cast, all bones were thrown
it has been predestined
we must wax, then wane
not will-o'-the-wisps
but all the same
ephemeral

Christa A. Bergerson

*And so our mothers and grandmothers have,
more often than not anonymously,
handed on the creative spark,
the seed of the flower they themselves
never hoped to see—
or like a sealed letter
they could not plainly read.
~Alice Walker*

To Hear the Silence

It is possible
to walk side by side
separately and together
like trees in a forest
that grow up
separately
     and together
         are the forest

Splendid is the forest
when we walk alongside
and separately
hear the silence

Lidia Kosk
translation Danuta E. Kosk-Kosicka

I słyszeć ciszę

Można iść obok
razem i osobno
jak drzewa w lesie
co dążą w górę
osobno
     a razem
         są lasem

Piękny jest ten las
obok gdy się idzie
i gdy osobno
słyszy się ciszę

Lidia Kosk
translation
Danuta E.
Kosk-Kosicka

Bolivar Heights
Patti Kinlock

Escape

Hank climbed the stairs to the back door of his house and knocked. The barking of the dogs on the other side rose in response. He had a key but figured it was impolite to barge in.

Rosaline was ready with an apology when she opened the door. "I'm sorry, but there wasn't anyone else to call." She led the way through the mud room, into the kitchen, and waited for him to wade through the pack of bounding dogs, twirling her wedding ring around a finger. Rosaline was always toying with something: clicking pens, shredding napkins, or playing with stands of her hair. He had stopped wearing his ring the day after he'd moved out but found he still kept his left hand buried in a pocket as much as possible when he was around his wife.

"I know Susie hates it when I ask you for help, but it's Sunday, and all the plumbing places are closed," she said. She turned to the four dogs. "Now, you hush."

The barking stopped. The leader sat back on yellow haunches and turned its doggy yawn into a human-sounding sigh.

Gettysburg Battlefield
Patti Kinlock

Rosaline wore the blue cashmere sweater she bought for herself a couple Christmases ago. Hank remembered her tearing gold wrapping paper off the gift box. It was just the two of them, and a ten-foot-tall blue spruce. The scent of dying pine filled the room. Rosaline had held the sweater against her chest and said in baby-talk, "Look what you got me, Honey-Bunny. Matches my eyes, hmm?"

Hank had taken another swig of beer and slurred something agreeable at her. After fifteen years of marriage, he had flat run out of gift ideas. Rosaline shopped; Hank's construction business paid the credit card bills. The perfect set-up.

Tonight, Rosaline wore a pair of tight jeans and tighter makeup. She kept herself in shape and was a good-looking babe for her age, but Hank wasn't in the mood for any of her games. He dropped his cap on the kitchen table, hung his jacket on the back of a chair, and headed for the basement door.

"Oh, take off your boots," said Rosaline. "They're all muddy."

Hank sat down and grunted around his belly as he bent to undo laces. He watched his reflection in the kitchen table's shine. Courtesy of Rosaline's daily applications of Pledge, no doubt. Lemon freshness filled his nose. He lined the boots up under the table. A hole in his right sock displayed the tip of a toe. Hank stood up and ran a hand through his graying hair. *Gotta get a cut.* Why did he always feel like a bum in his own house? At least he didn't live here anymore.

"Okay," Hank said. "Let me show you where the circuit breaker is for the well. That'll stop the water until you get a plumber."

A fresh volley of barking broke out as he got to his feet. The dogs, yellow and white muscular bodies mounted on ridiculous short legs, rushed at him. The boldest darted in and nipped Hank's ankle while the others circled and waited for an opening. Hank danced across the hardwood floor, arms akimbo as he slid on gleaming mahogany.

Rosaline clapped her hands, once, twice, and they subsided. She pointed down the hall. "Go on." Clicking nails punctuated by the occasional whine, the band of heroes departed for the living room.

Hank leaned against a wall and poked a finger through the fresh hole in his sock. He rubbed the sore spot on his heel. The skin wasn't broken. "Guess they don't remember me."

Rosaline stepped under the light. Her eyelids and the sides of her face sagged; she looked every bit her fifty-six years tonight. That meant it was time for another botox treatment, and he'd get hit up for a salon payment.

She put a hand on his arm. "Are you okay?"

Hank's anger eased at her touch. He shrugged. "There's no blood. I'll live." He opened the basement door and turned on the light. "Those dogs letting you sleep okay?"

Rosaline's hand fell. "Why, do I look tired?"

Hank gave up and thudded down the stairs.

Rosaline stopped at the top step. "I can't go down there. It gives me the creeps."

"Jesus, Rosaline, how can you live in this house and not use the basement?" He crouched as he walked forward under the low ceiling, flipping light switches as he went and trying to remember where the breaker box was.

"You should have thought of that when we bought it. I told you I didn't want a basement." He could picture her standing there, arms folded across full breasts—the finest his money could buy—leaning away from the open mouth of the door. "No, you didn't say a thing about a basement, one way or the other."

"I'm certain I would have, if you had asked."

Hank mouthed those last words, tossing his head back and forth in a parody of girlish peevishness. He flipped the breaker and headed back upstairs, brushing webs and dust from his shoulders.

Rosaline waited with his jacket in hand. "You better go. Susie's waiting." She helped him into the coat and gave his back a brief rub.

Hank felt ridiculous standing in his socks but otherwise dressed to leave. Couldn't she wait until he got his boots on? He fiddled with the jacket's zipper pull. "I gotta talk to you, Ros. Maybe now, huh?"

Rosaline's smile froze. "Is this about moving out? I can't until I find a job, and that's not easy."

"You still looking? I moved out over a year ago."

Her smile melted away. "Yes, I'm still looking. Give me a break. Nothing's easy after your husband leaves you for a younger woman." Rosaline's bob, yellow-white under the light, quivered.

Hank didn't know what to say.

"How old is Susie, anyway? Twenty-five, maybe twenty-eight?"

"Susan turned thirty-five last month. And we started dating two or three months after I moved out."

"So you're living with someone twelve years younger. That's pathetic." Rosaline's face was white and taut. "She's got her whole life ahead of her, probably wants a family. Which you've never been interested in."

Hank couldn't let her get away with that. "Says who? I know you felt bad after you couldn't get pregnant. I told you over and over that I was okay with not having kids. That wasn't the problem."

"I'm too old for you. You're seven years younger then me, and I couldn't stop getting old." She pulled out a chair and sat at the table, hugging herself. "Highlighted my hair, kept it blonde so it never went grey, starved myself, went through those surgeries…and for what? So my husband could leave me and shack up with some girl." Rosaline sniffed. "Well, I'm not signing any divorce papers. I don't care if you never come back. I'm not giving up my house." She smiled. Tendons stood out on her neck.

Hank's stomach curled up into a tiny ball. "Please, Ros." Why did his voice sound so weak? He cleared his throat. "I gotta marry Susan. I'm trying to do what's right. I always do what's right, don't I?" He sat across her, reached over the table, and took Rosaline's hand. He'd made her cry, but he had to keep going and say what he had to say.

Rosaline's head was down on the table, her face hidden by one arm, so when Hank nodded it was for himself. "I'm going to do what's right for Susan…and the baby."

Rosaline went still. "Baby? You and Susie?" She spoke into the table. "You and Susie are having a baby?"

"Yeah, me and Susan." He couldn't help it. He grinned. "Can you imagine? Me, a dad."

Rosaline leapt up, fists raised. Her face was dry. She flung herself onto the table, trying to get at him. "You son of a bitch! Get out, get out of my house!"

***

Hank stopped the truck, turned the engine off, and rolled down the window. Howls and barking floated down the hill from the house. He could hear Rosaline wailing against the chorus.

"Great job, you jerk," he said. *She'll come around*, he thought.

Liriodendron Mansion, Bel Air
Barbara Kirchner

Fog descended in a chilly blanket. Mature oaks on his property, trunks sweated black, marched up the rise through the mist. An overgrown lilac sprawled at the lawn's edge. He and Rosaline had planted it together for their tenth wedding anniversary—he'd dug the hole, Rosaline supervised. That corner of the property would be the perfect spot for a playset. *Next time*, he thought as he restarted the truck, *I will bring a shovel and a saw and take the old bush down.* He turned at the bottom of the drive and headed toward home.

May Kuroiwa

If there's a book you really want to read, but it hasn't been written yet, then you must write it.
~Toni Morrison

The Road

Dark skin,
weathered
by unforgiving wind,
her body breaking
in the sun.
She kept her garden
until the fever
and the county
took their plot of land,
making way for innovation and
Progress
and a straight, paved road
where their stalls once stood,
where people drove too fast
to get
nowhere
she ever wanted to be.
It was the 80s,
the horses were long since gone,
so she nursed him
and walked long miles
to the market,
pushing a rusted, metal basket.
Sometimes, they'd see her and stop,
offer to drive her,
and other times, invisible,
she'd walk—
calloused feet
in worn shoes—
back to him,
back to cold winters
and canned beans on buttered bread,
back to a life that didn't seem
so barren
until he wasn't in it.

Katie Hartlove

Winter Thoughts

Dr. Zhivago penned poems
from an ice castle, each thought
traveling on a breath of frigid air.
Snug in a candlelit room,
blanketed behind frosted window,
I yearn for that kind of dedication
Snow sheathes the ground
this last day of the year;
cars carry early morning workers,
flakes flutter in headlights.
Dawn lifts the shroud of night
beyond the hazy veil of Zhivago's breath
ice crystals sing his song

Deb Smith

Winter's Gown
Maxine S. Peter-Anderson

Winter Garden

Recognize the promise
Of a winter garden—

Press your hand against hard,
Unyielding ground
Frozen in the folds
Of its icy blanket—

And feel your fingers
Run through moist and eager soil
Throbbing with plump worms
And rich with nourishment,
Impatient to begin
The miracle of growth.

Listen to the clatter
Of brown leaves
And dried, hollow stalks
Rimmed with hoarfrost—

And hear the sweet, soaring song
Of robins as they glide
Through new-minted greens

And yellows and starry whites,
Thrilling in the caress of
Virgin petals and supple stems.
Breathe in the sterile air
Of frigid December
A visible cloud of
Biting coldness—

And smell the heavenly scent
Of lilacs wafting invitingly
From across the yard
Where a riot of tiny lavender blossoms
Cluster in delightful company
Waiting for you to join them.

Recognize the promise
Of a winter garden—

And perhaps it will inspire
The promise in you.

Danielle Ackley-McPhail

Frozen Pine Fingers
Maxine S. Petry-Anderson

*Courage doesn't always roar.
Sometimes courage is
the quiet voice at the
end of the day saying,
"I will try again tomorrow."
~Mary Anne Radmacher*

Unraveling the Still

Imprisoned by cold-packed wall, the door freezes.
Outside, the azaleas bow, crammed into iced
mounds.
The snow keeps coming down, sideways,
upwards.
Where the street was, wind howls, restructuring
the land.

On the second day, the first human appears in
sight,
planting heavy boots cautiously, taking in the
vastness.
Crystal-eyed, silent-still the whiteness turns
dazzling.

On the third day, the mighty icicles unravel.
Through the window glass, I catch their tears pure
enough
to drink. Lost for me on their way down unless I
freeze
them in my lens: the tips soften, sparkle, swell,
balancing
between solid, liquid, and air.

Danuta E. Kosk-Kosicka

Jo's Christmas Prayer

Melinda Jo was a six-year-old, jovial blonde
with blue eyes and a missing front tooth. She
was a poor child who lived in the Appalachian
Mountains with her parents and twelve brothers
and sisters. Though she never complained, she
had to wear hand-me-down clothes from her
older sisters and cousins that were tattered and
patched.

Her family lived in a house with two
bedrooms. Mom and Dad had their bedroom on
the first floor. The twelve kids had the whole
upstairs, which had been petitioned off with
quilts and blankets draped over ropes into
individual rooms. The older children helped the
younger ones, and each child had been taught
to respect the private space of their
siblings—so it was an agreeable arrangement.
And in the winter, the blankets and quilts could
be removed from the lines and put on their
beds if they were cold.

Most everyone in the hills needed some
sort of support to survive, and Melinda Jo's
family was no exception. Every month, Ms.
Shirley from County Services brought
commodities to hand out to those who'd signed
up for them. Each family received a large bag
of flour, a big bag of beans, a can of lard, a box
of powdered milk, and a large chunk of yellow
cheese. Occasionally, Ms. Shirley would have
a surprise or two—maybe a slab of meat or
some macaroni. But such surprises were rare.

Jo's mom knew the County Services agent
well, and they got along nicely. Shirley gave
all the people their fair share, and if anything
was left over, Mom would get extra.

Mom made bread from the flour, and Jo
liked it best when it first came out of the oven.
She'd ask her Mom if she could have a slice
with blackberry jam. The jam was thick and
sweet. They had made it from the blackberries
they'd picked in the summer.

One day, while with her mother waiting in
line to receive the County Service's food, Jo
glanced at the country store across the street. In
its window was a blonde-haired baby doll.
Even though she'd never had a store-bought
doll before, for Jo, it was love at first sight.

Granny had always made the girls in Jo's
family a homemade doll for Christmas as far
back as Jo could remember. She loved her
Granny and the dolls she made, but they were
for every day life. She could take Granny's
dolls anywhere she went, but the store-bought
doll was special. The store-bought doll with

her golden hair would stay in her part of the upstairs room and never leave the house. Jo would take good care of the store-bought doll and never let her get ruined. As soon as her eyes rested on the doll in the country store window, Jo decided that was what Santa would bring her for Christmas.

Even though it was spring, every night before going to bed, Jo prayed to Jesus to help Santa find a way to bring her the store-bought doll.

***

Jo was a kind, good, little girl and always helped around the house, dusting and sweeping, hoping to find or earn a penny or two. She saved those treasured coins for the country store baby doll just in case Santa didn't bring one.

Jo's parents had a vegetable garden, and the whole family was responsible for working in it. As told, Jo pulled weeds but was often caught pulling a new carrot out of the ground, too. Then, she'd grin, wipe the carrot on her dress, and eat the sweet orange nugget.

The family also had chickens that laid eggs unless the pesky red fox that visited frequently had them upset. Jo didn't realize it, but one of those chickens would be Christmas Supper unless her Dad shot a wild turkey on Christmas Eve. Dad was always going hunting to help provide food for the table. They had no freezer, so any meat he got either hung in the smokehouse or was stored in the springhouse.

The springhouse was where not only the meat, but the milk and anything else that needed to be kept cool was stored. Jo's Dad hoped he'd be able to trade some of his fresh game for a cow, so the family would have fresh milk every day. Then, they'd be able to churn the cream and have butter, too. Butter that would be oh-so-good on fresh bread with jam.

***

Come summertime, all of the kids in those parts ran around barefoot because their parents didn't have money to purchase shoes but once a year. Shoes were for winter, and most of the time, Jo's shoes were handed down from her sisters and cousins. But Jo didn't mind. And she didn't mind in the summer going barefoot because she loved to run through the long green flowing grass in the meadows and over the hills to her favorite spot by the river. Then, she'd sit or lie down under a big oak tree to dream. Sometimes, she'd dream about what she wanted for Christmas. Sometimes about what to get into later that day.

One day, as she sprawled under her favorite oak and studied the white fluffy clouds in the blue mellow sky floating by, she saw a cloud formation that looked like the baby doll she wanted for Christmas. Oh! But as she watched the image in the sky, it changed, and a different one appeared in its place. Jo sighed, rolled over, and decided to throw rocks into the river and watch the ripples slowly disappear instead.

She decided that today she'd tell her cousin, Gertrude, about the dolly she wanted for Christmas. Gertrude was six months older than Jo and was her best friend. Together, they often went on adventures through the hills. And quite often, those adventures found them together sharing secrets by the river.

That summer, like the summers before, blended into fall with the leaves turning red, bright orange, shades of amber, yellow, burgundy, and brown. Before long, they tumbled through the greens of the pines. The excitement was starting to rise for Jo and the rest of her bothers, sisters, and cousins because winter was coming, and Christmas would soon arrive.

***

Melinda Jo had a brother, Jimmy, four years older than she. He liked taking Jo with him when he went to the fishing hole to try to catch supper. However, he refused to take Gertrude with them because she was too noisy and the fish would not bite.

One autumn day, Jo made peanut butter and jam sandwiches while Jimmy gathered the fishing rods and got earthworms for bait. She carried the sandwiches, and her brother carried the fishing gear and worms as off to fish they went. Jo wanted to stop by her favorite spot to fish, but Jimmy explained that the water was to shallow for larger fish. And they would need at least six good-size fish to feed the family. She sighed but didn't complain as he led her to the fishing hole that had the larger fish.

As usual, Jimmy put the worms on the hooks and gave Jo a pole. Then, the two of them sat and waited patiently for the fish to bite. The dark greenish-blue water that their lines dangled in was very still. It had lots of rocks in it for fish to hide under.

After what seemed like forever, Jo felt a tug on her line, and she squealed with excitement. She could see a large trout flopping around trying to get away. Jimmy told her to flip the silvery creature up onto the grassy bank. The words had hardly left his mouth before something bit his line. At almost the same moment, both Jo and Jimmy pulled their fish up onto the bank. Her brother took the two large trout off the hooks and put them in a bucket he'd brought with them to haul their catch.

When they took a lunch break, Jo was so hungry, she quickly gobbled her sandwich and an apple she'd picked on the way to the fishing hole. While Jimmy finished his lunch, Jo told her brother that every night before she went to bed, she'd say her prayers and ask God to send her the store-bought doll from the country store window.

Prospect School
Barbara Kirchner

Jimmy smiled and patted her leg. He told her he hoped her prayers would be answered but not to get upset if she didn't get the doll. "Santa has had a hard time finding us here in the hills," he said. "Now, let's get back to fishing."

"Okay," Jo said as they threw their lines back in the water. She knew Jimmy wanted more fish for supper so all twelve kids, Mom, and Dad could have a good meal.

Before they knew it, Jo and Jimmy had caught six more large fish. With spirits high, they packed up their gear and the heavy bucket of fish and headed home. When they arrived at the house, they cleaned the fish and handed them to their Mom to cook. Supper was a feast. Everyone enjoyed such a fresh, tasty catch, and they praised Jo and Jimmy for a job well done.

***

A couple weeks later, things were looking very bad for Jo's family. Their father had made beds for each child to use, and some of the homemade beds on which the kids slept had broken. With the hunting season in full force, he didn't have time to cut down trees and remake several beds before winter set in. And so, the older girls came up with a solution.

McComas Institute, Joppa
Barbara Kirchner

They made sacks the size of the beds and stuffed straw in the bottom of the sacks near where the slates would be on the bed. Next, they filled the rest of the sacks with feathers they'd saved from their chickens or from their neighbors' geese.

Because of so many children, this was a work in progress when Jo's Mom talked to the local County Welfare Office and asked for help. Jo's family needed many items before winter, but most of all they needed beds. Mom was told there was nothing the County Welfare Office could do. The whole country was in a depression, and nothing was available for Jo's family.

Jo's mother felt she had to do something, so with small hope of an answer, Mom sat down and wrote a long letter to Eleanor Roosevelt, the wife of the President of the United States of America. She told Mrs. Roosevelt the situation her family was in. She explained they needed beds, winter clothes, coats, shoes, hats, gloves, and boots. As she mailed off the letter, Mom prayed that at least part of the items would arrive.

A couple of weeks later, a large truck pulled up in front of the house, and the driver asked for Jo's mother. Mom's prayers had been answered! What a wonderful surprise it was when the beds and all the other things she asked for were brought into the house. It was like an early Christmas.

***

By mid-December, it had gotten colder. Jo's Dad had several deer in the smokehouse. If meat ran short during the winter months, he'd try to catch a few rabbits. And Jo's Mom had jars of jam and preserved vegetables and fruit on the shelves.

Now, was the time to gather the family to go on the "pick the Christmas tree" walk. The whole family, except for the three youngest children and the oldest daughter, went to look for a tree. It was much too cold for the little ones to be out, and someone needed to watch them while the Christmas tree hunt was on.

On the "pick the Christmas tree" walk, the family sang carols as they trudged through the forest. The younger children pointed at every tree they passed and asked, "This one?"

"No, not that one." Mom and Dad smiled and shook their heads.

Finally, Jo's Mom and Dad answered, "Yes, I think that's the tree."

The anticipation was over. Jo's brothers took turns chopping down a beautiful fir tree that had limbs close together and stood about five feet tall. Then, together they dragged the tree home and took it inside.

Dad set the fir upright and put it into a stand. The time had come to make some new decorations. Jo, Jimmy and some of their older brothers and sisters made colorful paper chains, popcorn chains, paper doll chains, and stars of red, green, orange, white, and blue for the tree. The two oldest girls put candles on the tree before the rest of the decorations were hung. Then, Mom brought out the icicles she'd saved for many years. At last, the tree was decorated. It was Christmas Eve, and Christmas would soon be here.

The kids were so excited. Each hung a stocking on the mantle of the fireplace hoping to receive a few nuts and a piece of fruit. Jo knew it was an extra special treat to receive an orange in your stocking. They always seemed to be so expensive but so good. With a last glance at the stockings and tree, off to bed went Jo and her siblings. Even though it would be hard, they'd try to go to sleep hoping Santa would come during the night.

Christmas morning, Jo was the first one awake. She awakened the others, and they all went downstairs to see if this year Santa had been able to find their house in the mountains.

To the amazement of Jo, Jimmy, and their brothers and sisters—everyone had a gift under the tree. Jo screamed, squealed, and jumped up and down. There under the tree was the beautiful, blonde, blue-eyed doll from the country store's window that she had prayed Santa would bring.

Little did Jo know, Jimmy had told their mother about her prayers for the doll. And when Mom wrote to Mrs. Roosevelt, she remembered her hardworking little girl's dream of a store-bought doll. Jo's mother had included the information about the doll in her letter to the president's wife. When Mrs. Roosevelt sent the beds and clothing so desperately needed, she'd included the doll and other gifts for Jo and her siblings.

All that Jo knew as she held the beautiful golden-haired doll was it had been the most wonderful Christmas for the whole family that she could remember!

D.J. Mink

Alive with a Thousand Windows

My grandfather conducted the holidays
from his sagging leather armchair
surrounded by boxes of sweets,
cashews in dark blue tins.
His bay window, open
a finger's length even in December,
released the scent I guessed
must be Santa's own—cherry tobacco.
A pipe braced between his teeth,
grandpa talked trains on Christmas Eve,
whistle-sharp descriptions of the dining cars
on his beloved *Pennsy* run,
everything shaking:
white napkins folded into peaks,
an orchestra of silver utensils, coffee
black as a licorice pool.
I kept his stories preserved in tins
until my own words were ready—
poems alive with a thousand windows,
all the lights ablaze.

Shirley J. Brewer

---

*I paint my own reality. The only thing
I know is that I paint because
I need to, and I paint whatever
passes through my head
without any other consideration.
~Frida Kahlo*

---

*All art requires courage.
~Anne Tucker*

Gray Blue

The gray blue sky
spit snowflakes at me
as I stood above the place
that will be your house
for the rest of time

My lip
was sore from chewing it
to keep the tears from falling

My shoes
soaked up melted snow
where I stood
while taps were played

Barbara Weisser

Happy Hour

"Hi, Ron. Lovely weather." Michelle took off her dripping raincoat. Narrow opaque bands gathered at her feet and slithered across the laminated wood flooring. She was a striking figure at five-feet-eight, correspondingly large of body but with perfect proportions, with eyes the color of translucent amber and chestnut hair that fell straight to her shoulders. Ron never got tired of looking at her and often wondered if he had a crush on her. Michelle's looks demanded attention, but she was oblivious to the effect she had on people, especially men. "Where's everybody?"

"You're always first." Ron chuckled and handed her a scotch and soda. "This is one day I am happy to be indoors."

"Obviously, you're not the only one." Michelle glanced around. The little tavern overflowed with people. "There's no place to sit."

"Don't worry. The couple at the end of the bar is getting ready to leave," he said. "Come, Michelle."

Michelle wove through the crowd and sat on the stool. She kept staring at her drink while reaching for the peanuts Ron had placed in front of her. He glanced at her; she was completely engrossed in thought.

The three women met at the bar every Wednesday after work, and he had gotten to know them well. They often included him in their conversations, asking his opinion as they discussed their problems. The girls, all in their early thirties, had been friends since high school.

Ron, who was 31 and of medium height with a stocky build, resembled his Italian father with his coal black hair and matching eyes. He was tending bar at The Lazy Lizard while studying for his master's degree in accounting. Between college and working the night shift, he got little sleep. When customer traffic was slow, he used the time to complete some of his assignments. His schedule was hard on his marriage, and for Ron and his wife, graduation couldn't come soon enough.

Michelle checked her watch. "I hope Sharon's boss doesn't keep her late again. He knows we meet on Wednesdays for happy hour," she said, then sighed.

"Is he still trying to get her into the sack?" Ron's mouth curved into a wicked smile. "He'll never succeed."

The door opened, and Lisa entered, her hair plastered to her head, and her raincoat wrapped around her shoulders. She rose up on her toes when she spotted Michelle and pushed through the noisy crowd. "Hi, guys."

Lisa was an insurance claims adjuster who

spent much time on the road. Her outspoken approach often turned people off and, on occasion, had gotten her into trouble when dealing with clients. She had recently gone through a bitter divorce that had jaded her opinion about men. She firmly believed they were all jerks, except for Ron and her father, the only decent guys she knew.

"Where's Sharon?" She asked and then answered her own question. "That son-of-a-bitch must be keeping her late again. If only she would quit that damned job." Lisa took the seat next to Michelle. "Ron, I need a drink badly."

"She'll never quit because she desperately needs the money, and it's just not in her nature to fight back. She's not like you." Michelle spoke in a low, hushed tone.

"Until she learns to stand up to her boss, he'll keep on taking advantage of her." Lisa fluffed her short wet hair with her fingers and took a large gulp of her Bloody Mary.

Munching on a celery stick, she studied Michelle's face.

"Hey, are you all right?" Michelle turned her head, her eyes brimmed with tears. Lisa put her hand on Michelle's arm. "What's wrong?"

Michelle sniffled and searched for a tissue when Ron handed her a cocktail napkin.

"Thanks." She dabbed her eyes. "Lance has asked me for a divorce."

"What? But why?"

"As you know, we have been trying to start a family, and I haven't been able to conceive in spite of the fertility treatments." Michelle blew her nose. She closed her eyes and shook her head. "What a fool I've been! I've indulged myself in absurd hopes I could hold on to a guy like Lance without providing him with the children he wants and needs."

Lisa raised her eyebrows. She had always considered Lance a sleaze, certainly not the family man Michelle was describing. "Lance had been working late almost every day during the last six months. He was worried about our medical bills and said we needed the money, and I believed him. It turns out…" Michelle struggled with the words. "He's involved with an eighteen-year-old college student…and got her pregnant."

Lisa was speechless when Sharon rushed through the door, out of breath and dripping wet. She was short, with a round face accented by a small, upturned nose, and two dimples framing her mouth. "Sorry I'm late," she said and pulled the soaked scarf from her head when she stopped and stared at her friends. "What's the matter? Michelle, why are you crying?"

"Lance wants a divorce. The bastard got some college chick pregnant," Lisa announced, fuming with indignation. "Michelle, I'm so sorry." Sharon stepped closer to Michelle. "I can't believe it—" "I always knew he was no good," Lisa interrupted. "His new love better be prepared. Lance is not a keeper; few men are. Besides my parents, I know few couples who've managed to make their marriage work."

"Lots of people have happy, lasting relationships," Sharon replied.

"Oh, really? Look what happened to me…or you, for that matter." Lisa threw her hands up into the air.

Blooming Bromeliad
Vonnie Winslow Crist

Sharon dropped on the stool next to Michelle. She understood her friend's pain only too well. She and David had been married for three years when he had made his announcement.

They had met while studying at Peabody Conservatory. David, only a couple inches taller than Sharon, had been blessed with exceedingly good looks. He was the kindest, most generous person she had ever known. Their common interest in music forged a strong bond between them. They got married right after graduation, and David was accepted immediately as a pianist in the Symphony Orchestra. Sharon, who played the violin, was not so lucky and ended up taking a job at a law firm. Music was an important part of her life, and she struggled with the disappointment of not being able to find sustaining employment as a musician.

"Lance is no better than David," Lisa said.

"Please, keep your voice down, Lisa. David was confused. He loved me and still does…in his own way." Sharon hissed.

For a moment, Lisa stared at her friend with her mouth opened slightly, and then she said, "Do you really believe that he woke up one morning and discovered he was gay?"

"Can we forget about my situation for now and help Michelle with her problem?"

Forget-me-not
Jean Voxakis

Both women turned to their friend.

"Michelle, I know this is a terrible shock, and of course, you're devastated. Lance pulled a dirty trick on you." Sharon squeezed her hand, and smiling encouragingly, she said, "We'll help you get through this." She turned to Ron. "Give me a wine cooler and another scotch and soda for Michelle."

"When I got home last night, I discovered he'd already moved all of his clothes out of the apartment. I've tried so hard to make Lance happy, and I believed he really loved me." Michelle said pensively.

"If he did, the fact that you couldn't conceive wouldn't have mattered," Sharon said. "He would have agreed to adoption."

"Lance wants me to keep all the furnishings as long as I'll give him a speedy divorce. He's not the man I thought him to be, and at this point, I'm not sure how I feel about him…about everything. I guess I'm just numb…" Her voice trailed away.

Ron brought their drinks. "On the house," he said. "Look, Michelle, my advice to you is don't waste one tear on that guy." He patted her hand and hurried off to help a customer signaling for a refill.

"I have an idea," Lisa said. "Let's hire a hit man for Lance, and we'll tell him exactly where to aim."

Michelle gave Lisa a weak smile.

Lisa raised her glass. She looked fondly at her friends. "Here's to the future, a bright, happy future for all of us, and…." her voice caught, and then she added, "To our friendship, the one enduring substance in our lives."

"Cheers."

Karin Harrison

G

Veteran Soldier

She paints her face
With shades of brown and green,
Outlining in black—A touch of red
To show that she's bold.
She puts on her armor,
Lacing herself up
And tightening straps.
It feels like a second skin,
Snug against her body,
Sometimes with extra padding
Just to be safe.
If she is ready to kill,
She'll take out her stilettos,
Her secret weapon.
Her scars are hidden,
But they still throb
With pain from past wounds.
She has seen many comrades fall
And several betrayed.
The hour draws near—
Time for battle.
The bell rings—
She has been fighting for so long,
Yet she will never give up
On love.

Jennifer Wang

What If

I strained to hear it—and there it was. The ping of the elevator seemed to echo, ringing over the rows of cubicles as the last of my coworkers left for the ritual Friday afternoon happy hour. I had made some excuse to get out of it and was waiting for everyone to leave so I could pack up. I was looking forward to eating pizza on my couch as I watched my DVR'd shows.

I tapped my pen as I scrolled through my emails, searching for something to do. I sighed and swiveled around, then planted my feet and pushed off to twirl my chair. The light gray walls and dark gray carpet blurred by. Gray, gray, gray, swirling around me like a tornado. The squeak of my chair, faint hum of my computer, and buzz from the fluorescent lights were the only sounds at 6:30 on a Friday evening. The breeze from twirling ruffled my hair and wafted a fake lemony smell that not quite masked the odors of burnt popcorn and stale coffee. As I twirled, a bit of yellow caught my eye. The yellow post-it stuck out, the only spot of color in a sea of gray.

Call Meredith.

My sister had called me four times this week, but clients, projects, and deadlines all came first, didn't they? Well, I had time now. She'd probably be at happy hour herself and wouldn't answer.

Meredith picked up after two rings.

"Julie, hi! I'm so glad you called."

"Hey, Mer. Listen, I'm sorry I—"

"Jules, don't worry. Look, I have something to tell you."

I just knew it—she was getting married. Four years younger, but she had had a string of boyfriends since she was 10. I was 28 to Meredith's 24, but I knew, nevertheless, that she was calling me to tell me she was getting married.

"Julie, I—"

"Meredith, I know, congra—"

"No, no, Julie, listen to me!"

I sighed.

"Julie, I have cancer."

Have you noticed we go through life asking ourselves a series of "What If" questions? What if I won the lottery? What if I got fired? What if my car fell off a bridge? What if I had married him?

So when Meredith said, "Julie, I have

cancer," I wasn't really surprised because I had, in fact, asked myself that question before. "What would I do if something happened to Meredith?"

Don't get me wrong, I *was* surprised. I wasn't expecting that news. In fact, I didn't expect to hear from her until I saw her in three weeks for monthly brunch with our parents.

"What?" Maybe I didn't hear correctly. She had gotten engaged, right?

"Cancer. I have *cancer*, Julie."

"But I just saw you last week. You look fine."

In moments of extreme stress, time is supposed to slow as your life flashes before your eyes. I didn't find that to be the case. On the contrary, the quiver in my sister's voice; the distant hum of the air conditioner; and the tap, tap, tap of my pen on my desk all were unnaturally magnified.

I knew only two things after I hung up. One, my sister Meredith had cancer, and two, she only had six months to live.

Denial

The next thing I remember is sitting at the bar that evening for happy hour, arguing with coworkers about our new dress code policy, with no idea how I had gotten there. I kept thinking I had forgotten something. Did I need to buy milk or forget someone's birthday? It was a tickle fluttering on my neck, something I kept trying to swat away.

I woke Saturday and fell into my regular weekend routine. I went to the gym and grocery store, picked up my dry cleaning, cleaned my apartment, returned library books, chose a Netflix movie, and painted my toenails as I watched it. Monday found me back at work, catching up with coworkers. "What's new?" "Nothing, you?" "Nothing."

Three weeks passed before I found myself at my parents' house for our monthly brunch. Meredith. Cancer. *Right.*

Anger

I was late so everyone was outside. I walked down the hallway to the kitchen's patio doors. Passing a window, I glimpsed Meredith in the garden, stooping over the roses, a collection of red, pink, white and orange already in her hand.

I stopped to stare out the window at Meredith. You'd think I'd feel pity or sadness, but as usual, I'm just jealous. She's just so vibrant. Too vibrant, with her shiny hair and glowing skin.

Meredith bent down to pick another orange rose, and as her head started to turn towards me, I stepped back, away from the window. I didn't want her to see me watching her.

I had spent my life watching her. Smiling and waving to her from the couch with my book as she flounced out on the arm of her boyfriend or as she left when her friends' car horns honked. Reading her emails and Facebook posts to hear of parties, dances, and travels while I had books, exams, and papers, spending evenings watching movies with my friends.

On the refrigerator, posed family shots mixed with colorful, funny postcards from Meredith's travels. America's largest ball of twine, Las Vegas' Bellagio fountain show, the Statue of Liberty and Wild West cowboys caught my eye, making me smile. Then I realized there wouldn't be any additions to Meredith's travel wall, and my breath caught.

Ice slithered down my spine, quickly doused by hot water that turned to steam. Unfair. Unbelievable. Inconceivable. Ridiculous. How could it be?

She only had five months left.

Bargaining

I tucked my hair behind my ears, gulped some air, and opened the sliding door. Sheepish, I grinned at Meredith, and gratefully, she grinned back.

"Look at these," she said, holding out her flowers. "Aren't they gorgeous?"

I met her in the garden and gave her a quick hug.

"Mer, I'm a jerk."

She punched my arm and said, "I know." We both laughed, then started to cry.

I've always loved her but held her at arm's length. She wasn't as smart as I was and only had temp jobs, not a career. I repeated this mantra whenever I felt unpleasant niggles crawling inside my chest. Meredith went to Greece? I just landed a new client. She met a new guy? I was just promoted! I didn't have time for airplanes or dates.

I was happy with my life. Really. But I couldn't fathom it without Meredith. And with that one hug, my lifetime of jealousy didn't seem to matter anymore.

So I scrapped it all, pressed delete and started over. I'd be a better sister and friend. We had to cram a lifetime of memories into five months and couldn't waste one more minute.

Depression

I invited Meredith to dinner that Tuesday, then to a farmer's market on Saturday. She invited me dancing, then to a weekend in Cape Cod. More dinners, happy hours, and trips followed, slowly eating up the weeks.

Through the car rides, dancing, and fruity drinks, we slowly got to know each other. Like when we shared a bedroom, we had daily phone calls, inside jokes, and silent glances that told whole conversations. I went with her to the doctor and treatments, which we always

followed with a visit to Jahn's, an old-fashioned sweet shop that served banana splits and ice cream sodas. Just for that one meal, we'd let ourselves get sad and weepy, dabbing crumpled napkins to our eyes as tears ran down our face, desperately clutching hands while we tried not to hiccup too loudly.

It was after one such weep session that Meredith collapsed.

Acceptance

The next week, we had our ritual Tuesday night dinner in Meredith's hospice room.

We talked about her wishes—a red dress code for her funeral, along with a presentation similar to Liam Neeson's late wife's in *Love Actually*—an irreverent slideshow to rock music that celebrated her life. She shared her bucket list: visiting Turkey, sky diving, riding a mule in the Grand Canyon, and meeting Oprah. I told her how I hoped to be promoted soon.

Meredith frowned.

"Really, Julie?"

"What?"

"That's what you're looking forward to?"

"Well, yeah," I said. "What else do you want me to be excited about?"

"Oh, Julie," she said sadly.

Cylburn Magnolias
Danuta Kosk-Kosicka

She grabbed my hand and leaned toward me until her blankets slipped and the remote clunked to the floor.

"Promise me you'll do everything I can't. "

Meredith reached behind her neck and took off her necklace. A bright silver disk with "Live, Laugh, Love" etched on it winked at me in the light.

So, here I am, three months later, with one hand clutching my necklace while the other clutches the edge of the open jump door of the plane, the wind whipping my hair and my pants flapping against my calves. I took a gulp of air, stepped forward, and jumped.

Laura LaChapelle

Winding Tree
Jean Voxakis

The Fellowship of Trees

The summer my father died,
I began to study trees.
Sketching in my journal
oak and birch, I lost myself
in the communion of branch and bark,
the motion of a leaf before a storm.
I missed my dad's litany on our walks,
how he paused in front of each house
as if I didn't know the neighbors:
*Lou Mauro kills his lawn, can't tell
a rose from a weed. The Hannon's willow
needs a trim; their kids all moved to Denver.*
When my father was alive, we walked
beneath a canopy of trees,
our conversations shaded by green
in summer and spring. In autumn, our words
rustled like red and yellow syllables
eluding the rake. Winter
found us talking in cold moonlight,
our breath rising in twin puffs
toward the barren branches.
Those branches consoled me
on the walk I took alone
my dad's last day on earth.
Sorrow in every step, I walked
the tree-lined streets we knew,
listened to the sound of my father's voice:
*Shirley Squirrelly, never early;
our trees need pruning
all the time, a big yard's a helluva job.*
Who could explain Dad's words
captured and played back for comfort
by the miraculous fellowship of trees.

Shirley J. Brewer

Long Mourning

Oh, my dearest loving husband
Gone from me and from my bed
In my dreams, we chat and ramble
There are you, never dead.
Women, bring the shining myrtle
Light the candles, gray and red,
Let the waxes run together
Sing of him; he is not dead.
Years have gone, I light the candles
Still, in times of memory.
Stand, my friends, beneath the willow
Chant of love beneath the tree.

Marcia Kurland Miller

Lineage

My oldest self
Is a bequest to many of me.
I am dual, triple, numerous, more.
I am a multitude.
The center of me is not to be found;
It is not visible, not tangible, not audible.
Yet it sings, it vibrates, echoes, glows.
It teaches me of my past,
Advises about my future.
From dawn until sunset
My inner light glows small;
In darkness, its emanations
Guide the path of my dreams
So that Death can never find me.
I lived.
I live.
I continue forever.

Barbara Kirchner

The Cat and the Fireworks

At the first volley of fireworks,
unseen except for flashes
of lightening like light,
the calico cat sprang to alert.
leapt to the windowsill,
retreated under the bed,
then emerged and sprang to the
top of the bureau.

A low growl rumbled from
her belly—
a sound I never heard her make before.
Deep, rolling growl
sound radiating through fur
as she watched from
her patrol post
for the duration of the fireworks.

She became the cat in someone's bedroom
in London,
on the first night of the Blitz.
She became the cat distracted
from catching rats in the church
in Dresden,
as the planes rained down fire and boulders.

She became the cat cowering in the doorway
in Baghdad,
When the Americans bombed Saddam
back to his bunker.

All the cats
in all the arrowstruck, cannonstruck
cities down the centuries,
interrupted, startled,
terrified, growling deep,
feral, innocent,
instincts bristling.

Anne M. Higgins

Seeing Spots

Leftover raindrops spatter the
screen in my dining room window,
look like a kid's page of connect-the-dots
Either that
or all the constellations
on a gloriously clear night
Either that
or the road map
I've been looking for
as an escape route
Either that
or a figment of my imagination

Deb Smith

By Fortitude and Prudence (an excerpt)
Baltimore, June 1876

Rasheen turned the ring over and stared at the wisp of blond hair resting behind its jet stone. The trouble with living up to the expectations set by others, she thought, was that it only met with disappointment for all concerned. Daniel's reprimands still rang in her ears even though his image was fading from her mind as a dream dissipates upon wakefulness. She closed her fingers around the mourning ring, digging the seed pearl rim into her fingertips. He would certainly be displeased to see her sitting alone on a public park bench with her gloves tossed in her lap. Such behavior was simply unacceptable.

Her lips formed a rueful smile. Now she knew why her wedding ring had always felt so weighty. Along with the ostentatious yellow diamond had come the revered Langston name and all the responsibilities of keeping up the social facade that a life studded with wealth and privilege entailed.

Weary from her memories, she leaned her head against the top of the bench. Dappled sunlight from a nearby elm tree found its way through the black veil covering her face and warmed her skin. The whisper of human voices carried by the summer breeze mixed in the with the muffled clip clop of horse shoes hitting the street surrounding the park were a soothing melody to her ears. In the midst of such a tranquil atmosphere, she tried to forget the past and contemplate her uncle's offer. Though it was tempting, she would have to tell Uncle Frank to find someone else for the position.

She couldn't manage a teaching position and her responsibilities as the widow Langston. It was time for her to return to the Langston mansion. She had been away far too long. At her mother's insistence, she had come to stay with her family after Daniel's funeral for a few weeks, but the weeks stretched into months, and now, an entire year had gone by. She had to return. After all, she was Daniel Langston's widow. There were expectations to be met. She sat up and squared her shoulders. Back on her finger went the mourning ring. Back on her hand went the glove. Somewhere up in the branches, a Blue Jay squawked in protest.

She started to rise to leave but dropped back onto the bench when she saw a young woman push a pram down the pathway. As she stared after the disappearing figure, a familiar emptiness engulfed her but not for long. A persistent presence nudging her hand interrupted her gloomy reminiscences. Startled, she looked down at a large brown dog. The animal gave one last determined thump before placing his muddy paw in her lap.

"Well, hello there, fellow."

The dog put his other paw in her lap, raised himself up so that he was eye level, and then proceeded to push his nose under her veil and lick her face, knocking her bonnet askew in the process.

Struggling to move his paws back to the ground, she laughed. "Now see here, that's not very mannerly."

"Down," commanded a firm male voice before she could get the dog under control.

The dog jumped down and scurried off into some nearby azalea bushes.

Rasheen looked up at a deeply tanned face, crowned by thick ebony hair. The breath left her body, and for several long moments, she couldn't speak a coherent word. She recognized those handsome features, those cobalt eyes which had once offered encouragement and the slightest bit of indulgence. Her heart thumped erratically at the memory of a young girl's secret infatuation. Even now, the intensity with which he looked at her beneath those dark lashes completely unnerved her.

"Are you all right, Mrs. Langston?"

She sucked in as much air as she could and tried to focus on the present. He might very well be the most handsome man in all Christendom, but the arbitrary attitude of command he had just displayed irritated her.

"I'm fine, thank you just the same." She twisted her head toward the direction where the dog had run. The sudden movement caused her loosened bonnet to plummet from her head, its veil slipping through her fingers as she tried to prevent it from falling to the ground.

"Now look what you've done!"

Before she could lean forward to retrieve the errant bonnet, he scooped it up and held it just out of her reach for several long seconds during which his eyes caught and held hers. It was as if he was taking her measure, and she wasn't sure if she passed the test. Well, she was familiar with not measuring up, so he could take those mesmerizing eyes and go the devil as far she was concerned.

St. Michaels
Danielle Ackley-McPhail

"Mr. Reilly, are you going to give me my bonnet or stand there holding it all day?" She asked in the most aristocratic tone she could muster.

He handed her the bonnet. "I'm not the one responsible for your mishap."

"Oh bother it all!" she shouted as she threw the hat beside her on the bench after a futile attempt at returning it to her head. "I'm perfectly capable of handling a friendly dog without a gentleman's assistance."

His dark eyebrows arched in disbelief. "I didn't realize the animal was yours. I'm sorry to have disturbed you." Before she could reply, he tipped his hat, turned on his heel, and strode off muttering something about ejit blue bloods.

She regretted being so nasty, and if she were to be honest, it wasn't him she was angry with but herself.

"Can't even mourn properly. Just add it to the long list of failures," she whispered to the ghost of Daniel's memory.

She looked down at her dirty lap and decided she'd at least brush the mud from her skirt. After only one quick swipe, the dog come out of hiding and repeated his affectionate assault. She wrinkled her nose when the dog's wet fur came

Biltmore Estate
Iris
Mary A. Stevens

close. "Good heavens, where have you been swimming lad?"

Rasheen looked about to see if anyone was searching for a lost dog. Finding no one, she decided to walk home. Her dress was badly soiled, and she didn't even try to put her hat on but carried it at her side, the dog trotting after her.

Quite a few heads turned to look at the dirty pair as they made their way out of the park. Hopefully, she wouldn't encounter any of her late husband's acquaintances. It would not sit well with the Langston peers for his widow to be found in such a state of disrepair.

"Well, my good man, it looks as if you're coming home with me. What do you say to that?" The dog stopped in front of her and gave her his paw. "It's settled then. You'll have to be charming to my mother, but I think you're up to the challenge. I wonder if she is."

When they reached the back door of the Thornton home, Rasheen peeked inside to make sure her mother wasn't in sight, then took him to the basement where she and the Thornton maid, Mary, attempted to bath him.

"Miss Rasheen, your mother is never going to allow you to keep this animal."

Before Mary could rinse the soapy dog, he broke loose from Rasheen's hold and jumped out of the tub. He shook his body, slinging sudsy water all over the two women. Just as he was about to bolt toward the stairs, Rasheen dove on top of him, keeping her arms tightly wrapped about his neck. Together, she and Mary shoved him toward the tub and lifted his front section over the side.

"Miss Rasheen, this isn't exactly a lap dog."

Mary huffed as she somehow managed to place his back end in the tub while Rasheen held onto his neck keeping the front end in place. Once he was rinsed, they let him jump out again and dried him with some old towels.

"Now, you have to stay down here until you're completely dry. Mother's going to be more difficult to charm than I was." Rasheen patted the dog's head. "You'd better let me see if I can soften her up a bit before we introduce you. In the meantime, be a good boy, and I'll see what I can find for you to eat."

She bent down and threw her arms around the dog's neck. "Would you please give him some water?" Rasheen asked Mary over the top of his head.

"Yes, ma'am. He surely is the biggest dog I've ever seen."

"You aren't offering any encouragement, you know."

"I've none to offer. I know your mother. I don't think you'll win this battle, no matter how much you wheedle."

"Aw, Mary, have a little faith."

"Faith, I have plenty, but it will take more than a miracle to sway Mrs. Thornton."

"You're forgetting Granny."

"Even your Granny can't help with this one," replied Mary with a shake of her head.

Alice Bonthron

G

Eating French Toast
Union Station, 1959

Down the escalators,
we get on the train.

The porter lifts the bag.
Helps us up.

The train stops
Alta Vista Virginia.

Bakery box lunch,
Brought aboard.
Fried chicken and biscuits.

We were warned
about strangers with candy.

We consider the old lady,
the gum she offers.

We get off the train
High Point North Carolina.

Great Aunt and Uncle unload us
and our brown suitcase.

There is no bathroom in their house.
There is a pony in the barn.
We will stay.

Eating light bread,
if there are bugs in the flour
and no biscuits today.

Light bread or biscuits,
we will learn to sop a plate at dinner,

turn it over,
and come back to it at supper.

All this until Great Aunt and Uncle
load our suitcase,

lift us to the porter,
and back onto the train.

But before the train,
the biscuits, the pony

We enter Union Station,
turn right through the wide glass doors,

sit on twirling silver stools
at the white marble lunch counter.

French toast ordered.
Soft snow piles of sugar on top.
Maple syrup glazing the plate.

Then down the escalators.
Mom will worry.
Dad tells us who is in charge.

They kiss our sweet, slick faces, smiling.
Dad tips the porter.
A lift aboard.

Our hands holding tickets,
Their hands waving goodbye.

Cyndy Izadi

I would venture to guess that Anon,
who wrote so many poems
without signing them,
was often a woman.
~Virginia Woolf

Postcards

I was twenty and a full-fledged
hippie chick with long
curly hair, dressed in cut-off jeans,
and an Indian-print halter top.

Together with my best friend since 5th grade
Leaving on a cross-country Odyssey
to explore the USA
in a blue Chevy van.

Cheerful good-byes
were sprinkled with
fierce hugs, wordless kisses, and
cautions about flat-tires and hitchhikers.

Dad held a stack of postcards,
old and faded,
hand-painted and sepia-toned
of Mt. Rushmore, The Great Salt Lake,
and The Smokey Mountains.

He pressed them into my palm,
along with his fatherly trust.
"Ann, they're stamped and addressed.
Just drop a line to your mother
and me. Have a good time."

I loved him but inside
I was laughing.
Unable to figure out
why my frugal father would give me
postcards.

Yet Dad's postcards became part of a
weekly evening ritual and a lifeline of
connection.
Sitting at the picnic table
by the light of a Coleman lantern,

I sketched descriptions
of assorted characters,
inventive camping menus,
and near-misses with wandering bears.

Years later after Dad is gone
I find a sepia-toned card
of the Smokies, postmarked
St. Louis, Missouri, and
scribbled with my notes about
the swaying Arch across the Mississippi.

I feel the tether of trust
connecting me with my father.
The same heart-to-heart thread
that honored my decisions,
comforted me in despair,
and celebrated my joys.

Ann Bracken

The Sun Rises on Elmora Avenue

My family moved to our Baltimore row
house when I was four years old. I soon found
out that there were kids living in the house next
door. Their names were Sierra Sue and Debbie.
They had another sister, too, but she was a lot
older than we were. Debbie was only two, then.
Susie, as we called her, was my age. We all
became happy playmates, who fought sometimes
and loved each other the rest of the time.

We played hopscotch, jumped rope, skated
almost every day, formed secret societies, talked
to neighborhood dogs, and made friends with
other kids who lived nearby. As we got older, we
could venture a little farther from our own block
and begin to discover the rest of our enclave.

Our little neighborhood had some very distinct boundaries. Our house faced Belair Road. We lived just a few blocks from North Avenue, which was the Baltimore City line many years ago. Across the street was a huge cemetery where the Jewish people would come to bury their dead before sunset. We were bordered on the south by a railroad track. The track ran through a sort of chasm cut out of a hill at one end, but at the west end, the train crossed over Belair Road on a bridge.

Three blocks to the north, there was an old, old cemetery that was both overgrown and run down, and looked scary both day and night. People said it was only for black folks and was now abandoned. On the east side, there was an area that was enclosed by a ten-foot-high fence that ran the entire length of the four side streets that made up our little world. It was a private all girls Catholic school. On the property also stood a convent, which housed the nuns who taught in the school.

When our small enclosed neighborhood was built, it must have seemed to be on the outskirts of the city. All of the row houses were pretty much the same. Our blocks that faced the busy road were shorter than the ones that ran perpendicular us. The streets were narrow and had almost no traffic on them. Mornings and evenings, they were only used by the people who lived there as they went to and from work. They were all one way streets with names that spoke of open country: Ravenwood, Elmora, Lindale, and Elmley Avenues. And on the edges of these streets grew mature Elms and Lindens.

By the time I was nine or ten, I knew every inch of that area by heart. Each long block had its street, a small strip of grass where the trees grew, a concrete sidewalk, and then, the houses. Behind each row of houses, there were alleys for the trash men to pick up the cans and for people to drive to their tiny back yards.

A few of the Elms and Lindens had grown so large that they had cracked and buckled the sidewalks. The cement slabs near them were pushed up a few inches on one end. Some tree trunks grew over the concrete, and it looked like the trunk had melted or run down in a puddle and had been frozen. The imperfect areas of sidewalk made roller skating challenging and exciting. We knew where to jump over a big crack and where each upheaval would give us a lift. Those uneven sidewalks also caused many a skinned knee and scraped up hands.

Although Debbie and I lived right next door to each other, we never went to the same schools. Susie and Debbie got on the bus every morning and went to The Institute of Notre Dame School, which was on Asquith Street, farther into the city. I walked in the other direction to Brehm's Lane Elementary, P.S. 231.

Barbara Weisser

Trees Above
Vonnie Winslow Crist

Screen Doors and Kerosene Lamps

Our screen door to the porch squeaks. Not just a little tiny bird-like sound, but a real, full-fledged squawk. We have tried all sorts of oils, including WD-40, of course, and it still squeaks. The double metal-frame doors have something like piano hinges, and they are not easy to adjust. If that is even the problem.

Secretly, I rather enjoy the squeak. It isn't an unpleasant sound to me but, rather, brings back memories. My grandmother's screen door when she lived on Kennesaw Avenue in Marietta, Georgia, squeaked, and I know surely my many uncles had all had a shot at making the squeak go away. When I think back on it, I believe that at least one screen door squeaked at every house I have ever lived in and many I have visited. Perhaps it is the eventual duty of a screen door to squeak.

The squeaks always remind me of warm weather and going in and out so much and hearing the constant admonition not to let the

Curio
Danielle Ackley-McPhail

door slam. Those coiled spring wires would surely close the door but not at all gradually. Unless they were held up, they would slam. The proper technique, even with one's hands full, was to hold out a foot behind you when coming or going to catch the door and let it close softly. Little boys, especially, seemed to have a terrible problem allotting enough time to their entrances and exits to employ this technique, with predictable results: a slam, and one adult or another loudly commanding the child not to let it happen again.

My brother reminded me that the squeaks served as a very effective security system, too. The boys could not get in or out without announcing their presence, followed by a parental warning not to go out, a demand as to where the child had been, or an order not to slam the door, yet again.

Screens were not always taken for granted in the households of my childhood. When I was tiny, Grandmother Martin lived out in the country, and some of her neighbors didn't have screens at all. Evidently, there were not as many bugs then. Electricity wasn't necessarily everywhere, either. One of Grandmother's neighbors, Mrs. Loudermilk, I believe, had neither. Instead of electricity, she had a number of kerosene lamps that provided light for reading or sewing after supper. Those lamps had glass chimneys that shielded the flame and magnified the light from it. The chimneys collected soot from the burning kerosene and had to be washed every morning if the lady of the house was to maintain her good housekeeping reputation.

Grandmother used to tell the story that one morning Mrs. Loudermilk had an unexpected visitor. It was warm summertime, and all the windows were open. When the two ladies went into the parlor, Mrs. Loudermilk was horrified to see that she had failed to wash the lamp chimney earlier. Now completely undone, as she was offering her guest the best chair, she whisked away the offending chimney on the lamp on the table next to the chair and just pitched it out the closest window!

Every now and then, especially in winter, we lose power and get out the kerosene lamp that sits in a corner next to the fireplace in the Great Room. After power is restored, I never fail to wash the lamp chimney before it is put away. It's so easy to lose that Good Housekeeping seal of approval.

Lily Grace M. Hudson

If I'm honest I have to tell you
I still read fairy-tales
and I like them best of all.
~Audrey Hepburn

We Made Believe

Once upon a time, we thought
a bough could break,
a cradle fall, and you would hush-a-bye.
Baby, you didn't hush. You cried.
Remember when your father was
in the counting house
and how we waited with our wings folded,
baked into a blackbird pie.
We thought ourselves a dainty dish.
We thought could we fly from the filling
and sing
if only someone cut our crust.
From the cat that killed the rat
to the cow with the crumpled horn,
it all made sense then, didn't it?

Then Johnny was so late at the fair,
and still you waited for a bunch of blue ribbons
to tie up your bonny brown hair.
And remember your pumpkin shell?
In the end, it didn't matter how well
Peter kept you. Did it?
You can't say you weren't warned, Ladybird,
that your house was on fire and
your children all gone.
I told you, you were Wednesday's child
and full of woe
I told you what little boys are made of.

Barbara Westwood Diehl

Baby Clothes

Myra likes to buy baby clothes. Bright colors. Bold patterns. She likes fire engine red and navy blue. Yellow only if it is crayon yellow, not pale banana. She likes babies to glow.

Myra's children outgrew all their clothes. She had saved none of the sleepers her children wore or the sun hats with sea creatures and chin straps. The socks are gone. The sweater embroidered with apple trees is gone. Her babies grew into new and strange children, outgrowing Myra, growing back in time away from her. Bleached to cloudy blue and dry peach, like a photo left outside through day after day of sun and rain. They disappeared into large shiny snowsuits and fat scarves up to their eyes or under giant straw hats with satin ribbons like the little French girls in storybooks. She doesn't know where they are. She doesn't know their clothes anymore, where they are bought, or who makes them. She cannot tell them what to wear. Her iron is cold.

She should have grandchildren. That's the natural order of things. She knit, she sewed, she

mended. She tied, she buttoned, she snapped. Grandchildren are her due. Grandchildren to dress so that they are safe and warm and obviously cared for.

Myra knows that there are always plenty of bold baby clothes in the second-hand store. Happy, laughing baby clothes. Clothes with royal purple cuffs and collars. There are clothes for every holiday, too. Myra likes the costumes, especially pumpkins and ladybugs. Not the dime store kind but the handmade. She has a discerning eye, an eye for quality.

She would never buy the plastic, glittery high-heeled shoes a child could topple from. She doesn't even look at the tiny shirts stamped with cartoons. The characters change so quickly and are forgotten. Some clothes are classic, dependable. They never go out of fashion.

Perhaps some things in life are best forgotten. Hospital corridors that stretch on and on like a dream, peopled by doctor and nurses in pale scrubs and masks, with pale, sterile hands held upright, trying to tell you things. Things you know in your heart of hearts are lies.

No pale pink or green for Myra. No milk-stained pilly flannel, cloth only good for dusting and growing gray with oil. She would never take cloth like that to the second-hand store, much less buy it. She bought only the brightest whites and blues, appliquéd with toys.

In the park this afternoon, Myra sees a baby trying to crawl bare-legged in sparse grass. His fat knees push into soft clover and slip in the dirt. Myra wants to take the sturdy overalls with bright red knee patches from her bag and dress him properly. Babies need a strong cushion, corduroy or stiff denim, against the elements. They need a splash of color, so they can't be lost.

Earlier, in the grocery store, Myra had seen a baby propped up in a cart, wedged among packages of white napkins and paper towels,

almost indiscernible. She wanted so much to take the gingham bib from her bag, navy blue terry with the alphabet sewn on in bright plaids. She wanted the baby to stand out like a kite on a cloudy sky. As she dressed the baby in her mind, the cart moved quickly to the end of the aisle. Myra caught the mother's quick sour look before she turned. Poor child.

Myra looks from baby to mother. The woman isn't watching him. She is sitting on the bench with her eyes half-closed. Her bra straps show. She is wearing rubber flip-flops. Myra stares at the barelegged baby trying to crawl.

From her bag, she takes the good strong overalls with brightly patched knees and lays them on the bench beside the baby's mother. "A little something," she says, "for your baby."

The woman says nothing, only looks at Myra and the overalls, then back at Myra. No motherly recognition.

"He could cut his knee on a piece of glass." Myra says. "Or get bug bites." She picks up the folded overalls and holds them out to the mother. "You never know what will happen."

The woman scoops her baby up onto her lap with one arm. With the baby laughing, she lifts both fat legs with the other hand and looks at the knees. She blows a puff of air at each knee. The baby laughs harder and grabs at her breasts and hair to pull himself up, dancing on the frayed hems of her cut-off shorts. She play-bites him on his belly and cheeks. Myra sees spit on the baby and looks quickly for a clean handkerchief.

Her stockinged knees and low-heeled leather pumps are pressed tightly together. She peers through the bottom half of her glasses at the contents of her bag and pokes among the many necessities. "There it is." She pulls at a corner of cloth and extracts a handkerchief, edged in lace and folded into a tiny square. Smiling kindly, she extends the handkerchief to the mother.

"Wipe your baby, dear."

Again, the baby's mother gives her only an odd, blank look. For a moment, Myra thinks that maybe mother and child are newly arrived in this country, or that maybe, she, Myra, has journeyed to some foreign place. Her hand lowers slowly to rest on the handkerchief on her lap, palm up, covering the bib and overalls. In the brief moment, Myra looks away, confused, the mother puts her baby on her hip and walks away.

Wind ruffles the evergreens and fountain water spray. The handkerchief floats to the ground, falling on dandelions. It skips away through the park before Myra can catch it. Then it's gone.

Barbara Westwood Diehl

Not all of us can do great things.
But we can do small things
with great love.
~Mother Teresa

Braiding

Braiding strands,
her brown silky hair,
her life over mine,
mother's over hers,
mine over mothers,
with hands and fingers,
of generations of women,
back to countries
across the sea,
and
to fingers yet unborn,
yet yearning to braid.

Janet M. Lewis

Hope

Heavens from above open
Rain pierces like sharp knives

Free will is your weapon
God's plan, merely a blueprint

Cup always half full—
alternative; not worth mentioning

Trees grow tall like teenagers,
despite soil declared infertile

Quiet strength, even when the
universe is against you

When cold, search for warmth
When dark, search for light

Lauren Burke

Token
Danielle Ackley-McPhail

Flowery Speech

To be in the room with you
and to not say a word
makes me so aware
of my breathing.

Tense as a formal garden,
I am waiting for vowel
or syllable soil, to turn
the spade, to release
the blossom, caught
on the thorns of our
green and budded talk.

Rosemary V. Klein

Gloryblue
Maxine S. Petry-Anderson

The Love Story of Norbert and Mae (an excerpt)

Mae perched at one end of the sofa watching Norbert guide a dilapidated Hoover across scruffy olive carpeting. Thoroughly delighted by the routine and having no lower limbs suspended from the cushions, Mae never worried that her blind friend might accidentally vacuum her toes.

Retinitis Pigmentosa had snatched Norbert's eyesight in his mid-thirties; Mae had lost her lower limbs to vascular disease. Her unstable marriage of 30 years had ended in divorce, while Norbert, now 62, had never married. Two solitary lives…one handicapped apartment building.

"I don't know how you do it," Mae said, raising her voice above the roar of the vacuum cleaner. "You don't miss a spot." Elton John glasses magnified the spark of love igniting her heart.

Norbert flicked the switch, allowing the machine's growl to dwindle before flashing a smile in Mae's direction. "Whatever I do looks good to me!" he teased.

"Come." Mae patted the cushion loud enough for him to hear the gesture he could not see. "Sit next to me…take a break."

Unplugging the cord, Norbert wrapped it around the handle and set the old Hoover against the far wall. His faithful guide dog, a Golden Retriever named Skye, lifted lazy eyelids, ensuring his master was fine before returning to his afternoon nap.

"Thank you for helping around here today." Mae took Norbert's hand, guiding him to her. "I really appreciate all you do for me.""The place looks good, doesn't it?" Norbert smiled. "We'll clean my apartment tomorrow."Mae continued to hold his hand, watching that coy

G

grin envelop his tanned face as he sat next to her. Wisps of straight gray hair fell forward, hugging his high forehead. "You know," said Norbert, turning to face her. "I've never read your face. I have a picture of you in my mind, but if I touch your face, just lightly, I'd have a clearer image. May I?"

Mae shifted to face him, schoolgirl butterflies in perfect attendance. Norbert cupped her face gently, his wrists just about touching at her chin. He skimmed his thumbs along the bottom rims of her glasses, letting his fingers frame the opaque tops. Slowly, he stroked her forehead and temples.

"Are your eyes closed?"

"Oh!" Mae breathed, not knowing until that moment that she had stopped. "Okay, they are now." "You are lovely, Mae." Words spoken, Norbert traced her upper lip with his index fingers, letting his thumbs dip to her bottom lip, his touch a prayer. *I need to kiss her,* he thought. *What better image for my nights.*

"Your eyes are closed?" he asked again.

Mae nodded, unable to speak. His hands caressed her cheek bones, her chin. Butterflies lifted her small frame from the sofa, only to be caught in mid-air by Norbert's lips on hers.

Deb Smith

I, with a deeper instinct, choose a man who compels my strength, who makes enormous demands on me, who does not doubt my courage or my toughness, who does not believe me naive or innocent, who has the courage to treat me like a woman.
~Anais Nin

I'm very definitely a woman and I enjoy it.
~Marilyn Monroe

Art Nouveau Room

At Cumberland's Red Lantern
Bed and Breakfast,
we wake beneath
a portrait of Marilyn—her pouting
lips frozen in a kiss till
the poster crumbles.

Liz's violet eyes smolder
from the wall to our left.
Barbra, shy songster, peers
from between strands of hair
on our right.
Cher shimmers in beads and sequins
at our feet.

Slender nymphs lift a mirror,
recline on an ashtray.
And vamps from the 1920s pose
in black and white
photos by the door.

Owl light steals
between the mauve shutters, sparkles
the Tiffany blue-wisteria
lamp on the nightstand,
as my husband leans near,
whispers, "You are
the most beautiful woman
in the room."

Vonnie Winslow Crist

Yellow Pansies

There could be no mistake: the tiny bouquet was left for Margaret. After all, the flowers were tied together with twine, and hadn't Margaret just been saying she mislaid her last spool the other day?

Rachel, Margaret, and I stared at them for a good long while, bemused by their sudden appearance on the doorstep that morning.

"Who do you think sent them?" Margaret wondered. They were only yellow pansies, the same kind found hiding under the ferns of every shaded garden from Leonardtown to Baltimore but that didn't matter to her. She had never received flowers before, so she fingered the petals with as much tenderness as she would a bouquet of velvet roses.

"I think we should call him Mr. X," I suggested. "Until we know his name."

"How do you know it's a Mr.?"

"It has to be."

"But what does it mean?" Rachel asked.

The question sounded a little too profound, but that was Rachel. She liked to consider herself a profound sort. She lived by Austen and the Brontës and longed for someone to send her a love letter. The problem was we didn't live in an age of love letters.

"All flowers have a special meaning," she told us, happy to finally have a chance to share her knowledge of the romantically obscure.

Rachel came home that afternoon from the library, hugging a book to her chest. The title, *Language of Flowers*, was visible just above her fingers.

"There," she opened it and pointed to a drawing of a limp pansy. "Loving thoughts."

"But it's yellow, does that make a difference?" Margaret asked.

Not to be discouraged, Rachel paged through the book until she found the answer.

"Yellow means a secret admirer."

"Loving thoughts from a secret admirer. That's beautiful," I said.

For a few hours, Margaret blushed and hummed as she went about the house. I always suspected that despite Rachel's dreamy yearnings, Margaret was the one who would most deeply appreciate a charming gesture. By evening, though, she had stopped humming and used the twine to close up a sack of flour.

When she found another bouquet the next morning, Margaret went straight to Rachel.

"Does this mean anything?" she asked, holding out a bundle of purple striped carnations.

Rachel found the page a little too easily.

"I'm sorry I can't be with you, but you'll never know my name."

"Oh," was all Margaret said, then twirled a carnation in her fingers. If she was disappointed, she never told us.

"Mr. X. didn't leave those," I confronted Rachel as soon as Margaret went back to the kitchen.

"No," Rachel responded, not even trying to play coy with me.

"Why would you do it?"

"Does it really matter?" she closed the book and began to walk away. "It's not as though they speak the same language."

Hope Christine Stewart

---

*Make a difference about something
other than yourselves.
~Toni Morrison*

Missing Eunice

Poetry for breakfast,
strolling in the morning,
inspecting neighbors' lawns,
questioning.

Smiling though class,
you sipped tea, caressed words.
Yours was the last poem we heard
when you left, suddenly.

I pass your house,
empty now; neat, beckoning.
Reminds me of you collecting
details, opinions.

In your blue cardigan,
studious at eighty-two,
I looked up to your finesse.
Fine poetess, adieu!

Carolyn Cecil

Spiral Staircase
Vonnie Winslow Crist

Dreams in My Portfolio Redux

Wheels hum on the streetcar tracks
and whir with the new designs
twirling through my mind.
Dresses dance
energized by my dreams.
Fabrics cascade and swirl in my mind's eye—
The bias-cut skirt, the slim ruffle
perched above the elbow, hinting of sleeve
on a bare arm.
The dreams that live in my portfolio
yearn for the stage
blue velvet opera capes lined in persimmon silk.
A sheer chiffon gown refuses a slip
daring to reveal slender legs and graceful arms
demure and sensuous.
Designs for glamour-hungry ladies
longing to explode in a subtle riot
of sophistication.
The dreams in my portfolio
beckon meto the doorstep of my longing.

Ann Bracken

*One can never consent to creep
when one feels an impulse to soar.*
~Helen Keller

Mystical Leviathan
Mary A. Stevens

The Attic

Each time after she had written for a good hour or so, she would feel the sensuous afterglow of it; her senses dazed, a euphoric cloud in her mind. It was the relish that came from a deep raw hunger being satiated. When young students put the broad question to her of, "How do you write?" she leaned in close, her gray-green eyes taking them in as her thick silvery braid fell over her left shoulder and responded, "Passionately." Every year, her consecutive students would say how her devotion to her craft kept her young. "It's amazing. She treats her relationship to her art like a limitless love story that only grows over time…You can never try to put that woman in a box or up on a dusty shelf," one of her freshmen wrote in the '86 yearbook near her impenetrable portrait.

My grandmother had the admiration of generations ever since she began her career at sixteen during an apprenticeship with a local author. Her passion was fierce, driven, and sharp, though to those she loved, it was soft, round, and safe. My grandfather let me comb the chateau, picking those intimate things that reminded me of her life, according to me. Everyone was well-provided for after her death, but I was after something different than the others. For a woman of expression, she kept many secrets, and I wanted the explanations behind the explanations. I didn't take my husband or children with me to Ocean City on this visit to the house. I felt like I, myself, was a child again, alone and adventurous, searching for a world I wasn't meant to find. My hands stroked the surface of the rose-hued diary as I closed my eyes imagining her intense eyes watching the private words she wrote. I didn't open the diary, but as I replaced it to its drawer in the nightstand, a photograph tumbled out onto the floor. A black-and-white picture of her at twenty-one stared at me with a mischievous smile. Vivacious and attractive, she looked like she knew something that everyone else didn't. She was never one to discount signs, and this seemed to me like a sign from her that it was alright to continue my journey of exploration.

I had already seen the scrapbooks filled to the brim with memories…loves ended, loves begun, rights and wrongs done and undone. She sat next to me on the guestroom bed and showed them to me at the ripe age of thirteen when I was able to appreciate their significance.

"I've always loved the past too much," she told me as she stroked my hair. "I learned to live in the present, but I suppose it's simply an ailment of writers that we are always looking to glorify that which was. That's when our realizations come, and we've learned about ourselves…after the moment passes."

Now, I wonder if she's reliving that very moment with me because it's our shared past. The bed linens I was sitting on, the curtains, the rug, all of it still had her signature scent of musk, sandalwood, and lavender. It was in the air of everywhere she frequented, in all her clothes, and accessories that she let us borrow. Her close friends spoke of the comfort it gave them, yet she was always surprised when they told her about it as though she couldn't notice it herself.

Leaving the bedroom after I'd returned the photo and the diary to the drawer, the door of the hall closet caught my eye with a strange, ethereal pink glimmer upon its glossy surface. It was fleeting, but the rush of memory was there. I'd always dreamt of the ladder in that closet. It led to magical worlds one step beyond my imagination. It was whatever I needed when I needed it most, and somehow my grandmother was always there. But not as an elderly adult, as a child my age. My palm rested against the wood. My other hand clasped the golden handle but lacked the courage to turn it.

I closed my eyes and opened the door. Cashmere coats tickled my face and the smell of soft leather brushed against my nose. The white ladder was there; always tucked to the side but ever present. Relinquishing reason, I climbed it. There was a small hole at the top of the closet, scarcely big enough for my fist to fit through. I wondered how I had ever fit through it, even as a small child.

I decided to make it my intention to make it through the opening to the three rooms that had always existed in my mind. The sheer physics of it didn't matter. I would find a way. When I felt ready, a large panel slid open that I hadn't seen before. A petite hand a good deal younger than mine extended itself toward me. I recognized the child immediately as my grandmother.

"This place was always here for you," she whispered. "You could always fit as long as you wanted to." The long curtains of golden hair framed the rosy cheeked face that supported the large, inquisitive green eyes. She was all in white.

The three rooms of my dreams were there. There was a middle with soft light green carpets and white shelves filled with books. They weren't only the books my grandmother had later written in her lifetime, they were also the books that had inspired her from the very beginning of her life. I sat easily on the floor touching the old volumes and thought the thoughts that must have crossed her mind while she read them. I saw the world for a moment through her eyes. I saw the deep reds and purples of magic gardens and teacups, the greens and gold of foreboding forests, the characters that existed amongst nature's secrets. There were winding towers with princesses at the top, fairies coaxing in the seasons, and purple cities with moving sidewalks and ancient buildings ajar with ghosts flitting in and out.

She reached for my hand again and drew me toward the second room. The walls and ceilings were painted midnight blue. These were the toys of her childhood, the primary yellow, blue, and red that comprised her sense of adventure. Everything from dinosaurs to virtuous heroes in Halloween costumes lived here. She sat on the floor while I examined the plastic bins full of her play things. This felt like her tomboyish side that almost no one knew existed.

The third room she led me to was draped in shades of deep pinks and peaches. She looked older now, more like the vibrant photograph I had stumbled upon earlier in the bedroom. In here was the history of her great loves and how they'd interlaced themselves with her memories to churn out inspiration of what love could be. She stood to one side, a hint of mischief in her eyes. I knew that she was letting me be privy to her secrets, and somehow, she didn't object when I read letters, handled the roses, or peaked inside the lockets. I felt her life force in this room as well. It had simply matured further here. I found heartaches that were never completely resolved but forgotten and laugh out loud ridiculous scenarios that I couldn't imagine her being in, in the first place. There was a great love in here that never ended, and I could feel hints of my grandfather in the room.

When I had closed the unseen collages and finished seeing the running films of flickering moments in her life, those on ice, those in summer caught by chance, and those spanned years, she rose up to take my hand again. I had seen what she wanted me to see. She embraced me, and I felt that I knew her then more than ever before. Her mysteries were part of the legacy she left for me.

I smelled her perfume and filled my heart with it. My face pressed into it and felt a plush resistance. My eyes flickered open, and I realized that I had fallen asleep in my grandmother's bedroom. The photograph that I dreamt I had returned to the drawer lay beside me.

"Did you find everything, Abby?" My grandfather's question was hopeful. He wanted to give me what I wanted of hers, but he scarcely let anything go, either. My arms were empty spare for the photograph.

"Yes, I did. Grandpa, did Grandma ever mention the attic? I know it isn't finished up there…the ladder leads to nothing, but—" I cut off my sentence when his eyes flickered with recognition.

"Oh, yes. In fact, she was the one to tell me about it first. She had a dream while we were in the process of buying this house. In the dream, there were finished rooms up there. When we next spoke to the owners, they laughed at the coincidence because there had been three rooms up there. They belonged to their children. The original roof had just about been torn off in a hurricane while the family was away. When they were rebuilding, they decided to leave the new attic unfinished and moved the children's rooms down to the second floor for safety reasons. Why, Abby? Did she mention the story to you?"

"In a way…"

"I was always astonished at the bond you two had."

"Have, Grandpa…the bond we have."

Nicole M. Bouchard

Entering the Unrevealed Estates

Your words are more carefully
chosen, difficult to understand
at first glance, well-suited to disguise.
The small flowers, leaves, tendrils
transmute into the thin thread
or the thicker line on which you tie knots
and seed pearls. Taken by a reader,
they grow or at least stir.

Danuta E. Kosk-Kosicka

G

Sky Stories

White cumulus clouds
Swim languidly eastward in the quiet sky,
Like floating mermaids
Or a pod of sleeping whales.
They are akin to my thoughts,
Which meander through my mind
To form words, assemble poems,
Or phrases of things I want to say.
They arrive slowly, softly, quietly,
Building a scattered pattern against
the endless void.
And while I am seeing them in my vision,
I must record them as they happen,
Or they will float away
In the lazy tides of intangible blue.

Barbara Kirchner

The Poet-Birds: Nightingale

Sings mighty sweet
alone in the hedge
never to publish
beauty unfolding
for only herself
the love
she never had
closeted within
breast and brain
song held
beneath this bush
where rosebuds swell.

May Kuroiwa

Humble Pie & Similes & Metaphors

Liking your own poetry
Is like liking your own cooking.
You grow fat, self satisfied, smug.
Then, suddenly, a simile is a casserole curdled
In heavy cream, bland, untempered.
A metaphor crumbles out of the pan,
Falling with the other broken cupcakes.
Morbidly, a soufflé wilts,
Suffocating in its own hot air.
What recourse, poet-cook?
Break the pen, rip the paper.
Throw the spatula from your hand.
Toss every morsel through the back door.
Let the dogs feast on what remains.
Give yourself up to pizza delivery.
Don't mention this poem again.

Cyndy Izadi

Doll Baby
Patti Kinlock

Writing

The pen moves away.
Stroke by stroke, I form the words
Hidden in my heart.
I see what this poem is,
And it is no good to me.

Jennifer Wang

Soul Stealer

A man with a digital camera
turned casually behind him
capturing the living city
stealing a pretty face

Danielle Ackley-McPhail

Cloth Merchant
Wendy Hellier Stevens

Mosaics

Single, rough-edged, misshapen
Arranged one by one—meticulous
As the artist's calloused hand
Feels the danger of Creation
Collisions of color and shape
Every choice, every consequence
All life's longings
Even death's stillness
Births beauty from the broken pieces
Of discarded things.

Joan Donati

Picasso's Insomnia after His Final Self Portrait

Midnight in the emerald garden
And I long for the moon to drown
Me in its shadow, the sky to soothe
Me with its blackness, the stars to light
up the unshaven stubble of insomnia,
heavy and brown like mud.
If I could dream, my body would race
Backward with the swiftness of the Seine.
I'd dance with a barefoot maiden
In a cornfield, my green forehead
Obscured by a wide straw hat.
I'd inhale the apple of her hair,
See the lake mirrored in her eyes.
I'd strut in the willows, limbs nimble
With the greed of youth.
Still awake, I find sleep slow-footed,
dragging its shackles behind.

Mary L. Westcott

G

A Little Magic

Some mornings, I wish I could wake up and be more like Ian, less like myself. Not that I want to be seven again—those grimy hands, those missing teeth—but I wish I had his perspective on life or at least the imagination through which he experiences it. I am not the first to make such a wish; didn't Picasso comment on this frequently? "All children are artists," he said. "The problem is how to remain an artist once he grows up," and "It takes a long time to become young." If I were more a time traveler and less an anxiety-prone mother, I might find ways back to my so-called inner child, but she was an anxious thing, too, not inclined to see the magic in the mundane.

Watching Ian's imagination at work, I realize how far I've come from being able to marvel. We have been reading the Harry Potter series and are on the fourth novel; although most of the vocabulary is beyond Ian's ken, he seems to follow the plot, which he reinforces by watching the DVDs over and over. (When we read the first novel, which was quite a journey for a 7-year old more used to 20 page picture books, he would occasionally interrupt by sweeping his arm from side to side and saying, "All of *this* because of a cat in the road," an early scene featuring McGonnagall and Dumbledore from which the entire narrative emerges.)

Recently, he told me that he wanted a magic wand and drew a picture of the stick he had in mind, suggesting that Erik could make one for him. I went online and Googled magic wands, which can be purchased at great expense in all manner of artsy materials and configurations. But the other morning, Ian rounded up Frosty, his Westie, and set off for the woods, returning a while later with several sticks.

"This is my wand," he said, holding up a heavy twig, about six inches long, with a narrow point. "These are for Frosty."

He has since roamed the house, pointing his stick here and there and muttering things the rest of us can't hear or understand. He has memorized Potter's spells—*Expelliaramus*, he whispers, or *Expecto Patronum*. He holds one end of the stick against the dog and murmurs secrets to him. He holds the stick like a quill and writes invisibly on papers spread over the dining room table. Last night, while I was brushing my teeth, he used the stick to flick the bathroom lights on and off, shouting, "Lumos!" as he did. I am charmed by his spells—courtesy of JK Rowling—and his quest to find magic in our house.

When my five older kids were little, they must have had similar moments of wonder and delight, but I was always so busy dealing with the quotidian and the groceries, with laundry and dinner, that I never took time to notice. I vaguely remember things they did when they were at play: The toy soldiers melted on the baseboard heaters to make them look as though they'd gone through battle; the dolls dressed and arrayed at tea parties; the dress-up gowns which made all of them, even the boys, princesses. But mostly, I was too busy to notice, much less to admire the way they could rely on imagination and a few props to play for hours. In any case, I was always urging them on to the next developmental milestone, another bit of independence, and usually did not have the patience or the energy just to observe.

As I write this, though, I remember one incident of sheer magic, courtesy of Alyson, who must have been four the day she came screaming down our long driveway, shouting for me to hurry, hurry, hurry. Panicked by her cries, I raced from the house. "At the top of the driveway…hurry, Mommy, hurry," she said. She whipped one arm around in a circle and raced ahead of me, her short little legs making time as she flew. It was dusk, and the other kids were running around in the woods, playing on the tire swing. No one seemed injured; no one was

fighting. I could not imagine what was wrong.

Aly stopped short at the mailbox and gestured at the sky, where the sun was setting in a frenzy of purple and red; vivid colors shot through the clouds in an unusually fantastic combination.

"It's the most beautiful sunset ever," she said. "Look at it, Mommy, look."

I like to think that I must have looked for more than a second, that I must have forgotten about dinner or a work project or whatever chore was at hand and took a moment to appreciate the sight with her. Chances are I did not, although I remember the incident so well and often think of it when I see Alyson now, 17, still a little dreamy, with enough imagination left to daydream about movie stars and fashion shows. I am trying to remember that we each carry a little stick somewhere in our hearts and minds, and that if we think to use it, there is magic yet to come.

Janice Lynch Schuster

Remember, Ginger Rogers
did everything Fred Astaire did,
but backwards
and in high heels.
~Faith Whittlesey

I found I could say things with color
and shapes that I couldn't say any other way –
things I had no words for.
~Georgia O'Keeffe

Life Underground
inspired by the bronze statues of Tom Otterness

They lurk
In the station
At 14th and 8th
Deep beneath
The city streets
The demifae
Masquerade
As artwork
Ancient power
Cloaked beneath
Antiqued brass
Full, round
Gentle curves
Hold the illusion
Of softness
Cute, formless faces
Betray nothing
But on the sly
Black-dimple eyes
Flatten into dashes
Conspiratory winks
Only I spy
The slight bow
Of their mouths
Shimmer
With the ghosts
Of impish smiles
As I hurry by

The magic of the city
Couched in casual sculpture

Danielle Ackley-McPhail

Elevator Kaleidoscope
Patti Kinlock

To Bead or Not to Bead

"Where is Lachesis?" Atropos asked, cutting another thread from the current tapestry on the loom. The *snip* was clean, but she felt the thread catch on a burr and turned to hone the blades of the shears. She hated causing unnecessary pain. It was bad enough she ended the lives of everyone who walked the earth and many of those who did not. And Zeus help her if she frayed a god's thread while making the cut: she would hear about her clumsiness for an eternity.

Clotho looked up from her spinning wheel, guiding the reeling thread with a practiced hand. "Lachesis said she had an errand to run."

"But I have additional threads to sever this morning," Atropos said, crossing the marble floor to look out the spacious window. Far down the mountainside, the city of Athens awakened to the first rays of sun. "I hope she doesn't delay too long…lives are in the balance."

"Lives are *always* in the balance," Clotho said, guiding a particularly dense clump of wool onto the wheel. "That should prove interesting," she mumbled, watching as the wheel produced a thick fibrous strand on the other end.

Atropos frowned when she saw the broad strand but didn't comment. Instead, she said, "Lachy should have planned this better. What did she say she had to do?"

"Purchase some beads."

"Beads?"

Lachesis walked in the door. "I'm baa-aaack," she sang. "And, *by Zeus!* do I have an idea for how to spice things up."

Atropos looked down at the present tapestry with its tangled lines of life, some long and old, the thread thin and stringy; some cut short, as fat and vibrant as if the life just slipped off Clotho's spinning wheel.

She looked up at Clotho and had to bite her lip to keep from laughing. Clotho rolled her eyes in time to the spinning wheel and mouthed "excitement."

Atropos understood. What could be more exciting than spinning the thread of life mortals *and* the gods; weaving their lives together in harmony and despair; and then snipping them off…extinguishing lives as necessary?

"We have talked about your ideas before," Atropos said. "And we decided that everything works just fine the way it is."

"*You* have talked about my ideas before," said Lachesis. "I've never agreed with either one of you." She turned to Clotho. "You, my dear, could have so much free time on your hands if you simply mechanized."

"But think how bored I'd be with nothing to do," Clotho said. She changed the subject. "Were you successful in finding what you wanted in the market? I'm not certain beads are a good idea."

"Of course they are!" Lachesis said, moving across the room to the worktable by the window, rattling a clay jar of beads as she went. "Just think of what we can do with these."

Sea Horse
Vonnie Winslow Crist

Lachesis spilled a hundred or so beads onto the table. Large and small, clay, wood, glass, gemstone, steel—a myriad of choices, scattered across the tabletop with a sound like hail on the marble tile of the outdoor bath. A gleaming black bead, the size and shape of a date, skittered toward Atropos, losing speed but not enough to remain on the table. It toppled over the lip of the work surface into Atropos' waiting hand.

She caught the cool bead in her palm and closed four fingers around it, looking to Clotho for assistance.

***

Clotho looked down at the spreading beads but not before she caught the look of desperation on Atty's face. She wondered, not for the first time since Lachy said she had an errand to run, if she should have put her foot down this time. Would that have made a difference? Lachesis seldom listened, but Zeus might have been convinced to see the folly of her actions. He interfered even less than Lachy listened, but he also knew the history of her *ideas*. Lachy's experiments had not always turned out for the best.

Clotho turned to stare at a tapestry hanging on the far wall, a short project, compared to the many others they'd created through the ages. She insisted it remain hanging in this room, unlike other finished projects, as a reminder to what could happen when the three of them took chances with the weave.

Beautiful, silken threads in a rainbow of colors marked the beginning of the weave; colorful, light like a veil, the intricate pattern woven so ingeniously that individual lines blurred, impossible to see where one thread entered and another left. The pattern changed at the end of the tapestry, where Lachesis forced a change: a thin, dark strand woven among the lighter, airy colors. Yes, Clotho agreed, it *had* created striking contrast, but less so than the hacked-off ends where Atty, unable to keep up with the demands of the pattern—her scissors unable to cut through the lot of them cleanly—took to the tapestry with a hand axe, severing the threads in clumps.

Pompeii, she thought. *Beautiful Pompeii. What a waste.*

It amazed her that the gods insisted Lachy possessed the best temperament for weaving. Surely someone more stable, like herself, for instance, would be a better choice. She preferred to believe that their reluctance to remove Lachy stemmed more from tradition than from their actual belief in her skill. And the gods stick to tradition like Zeus to nymphs, for without it, where would they be?

The room was silent until Lachy clicked together three green beads in the palm of one well-manicured hand. Waiting.

Clotho felt herself flush with the embarrassment of being caught woolgathering. She cleared her throat, loathe to ask the question. "What's your idea?" she asked.

Lachesis bent to the work table and plucked

a dark thread dangling from one edge of the table and a vibrant orange thread from the other.

"No!" Atropos yelled, just as Lachesis slipped them through the bead and made a knot.

"Macrame!" she said.

Kelly A. Harmon

Defeated Women

It came that the people of Melos, resisting a distant master, had not been willing to become allies to fight a war. No island could be allowed such independence. That summer of 416 BC saw the Athenians rowing their triremes through a becalmed sea. To the south, the island of Dorian Melos awaited their invasion. Three thousand men laid siege to the walls of the city amid the green of pines and the silver of olives. With no military power, by fall, Melos had fallen. All the Melian men left standing were massacred, the women and children sold into slavery. Thucydides devoted twenty-six chapters in his *History of the Peloponesian Wars* to the Melian Dialogue, a detailed description of the nature of this crime of arrogance. *Hubris*, that sin of pride which points to the downfall of humanity.

Shaken by this event, Euripides reflections on the sufferings of conquest and war brought him to create one of his greatest masterpieces by the spring of 415 BC, *The Trojan Women*.

Going back ten centuries from his time, he found inspiration in the taking of Troy by the armies of Agammenon, the glory of the Greeks' proudest conquest. With one turn of the wheel that great victory is transformed into defeat, shame and blindness, and a world turned dark with sorrow. There are no genuine heroes; instead, *The Trojan Women* is the story of the vanquished, of the women and children left behind.

In a world where women had no voice, Euripides was the first to create a play where women spoke, reasoned, and saw the world in all its ferocity. However, Euripides was not interested in women's rights. The play was performed for men and acted by men, as women were excluded from the theatre. Yet it stands as one of the most powerful portrayals of women's dignity in front of predestined calamity.

The living drama rests on four figures clearly defined. The chorus of captives in the background are the half heard voices.

Hecuba, queen turned now into slave, raises from the ground at the clearing of the day. Her husband's body has been defiled. Her sons have been killed, her daughter Polixena has been wastefully sacrificed at the tomb of Achilles, and in the end, even her infant grandson will be dashed to death.

"Endure and chafe not..." [L.100] she tells to herself. And through this endurance she becomes the embodiment of all those mothers who have lost wars. Those torn by the loss of their children, their husbands, their grandchildren. Those who have survived enraged and hopeless and think the gods have forsaken them.

Cassandra is the priestess cursed with the power of unheeded prophecy. To the horror of her mother Hecuba, Cassandra is allotted to be Agammenon's concubine. But the prophetess sees this vision of Agammenon's murdered body, and beside him on the wet rocks, she sees herself dead and outcast. Her desecration leading to the ruin of the enemy. Joyfully, she consoles her mother, "I shall kill him, mother, I shall kill him, and lay waste his house with fire as he laid ours, my brethren and my sire shall win again." [L359-360]. And thus, she goes forth to what is appointed. A Phrygian woman triumphant in her hate.

Helene, who has been the cause of the war, paradoxically is the only one who will save herself and continue as a queen. When the

deceived husband Menelaus appears, he is infuriated. Then he sees Helene, beautiful and splendidly dressed, and his passion rekindles and he hesitates.

Hecuba and the chorus of captives who are dressed in tatters and have suffered every degradation expect the Spartan to punish the errant wife. Helene unrepentant argues her case, "…to be a toy of the gods…abducted against her will…ruined by her beauty, and damned by those who should have given her a garland to crown her head." [L 995]

Hecuba turns in rage, accusing Helene of having made her choices and wantonly lusting after Paris. [L 1005] "You ran riot in the halls of Alexander and luxuriated in barbarian customs…And look at you now dressed to the hilt, looking shamelessly on the same sky your husband does, you despicable woman. You should have come without airs, dressed in rags, and trembling with fear, your head shaven for shame, and shown more modesty than audacity before the husband you wronged." [L. 1020]

The chorus of captives exhorts Menelaus, "…show yourself worthy of your ancestors and punish your wife. Be a brave foe to your enemies and by her death erase this blot on womankind." [L 1030]

"When we get to Greece she will die a terrible death." [L 1035] Menelaus promises. Yet, he holds Helene affectionately against his body when he carries her to his ship. So Helene survives and goes back home to become again a queen.

Hector's widow Andromache is brought with her child Astyanax in a wagon loaded with spoils and Hector's weapons and armor. She has been allotted to Neoptolemus, the son of her husband's killer. Andromache epitomizes all the virtues of a good, obedient wife, "…I stayed home…my tongue was quiet, and my eyes modest." [L 650]

The memory of her dead husband will accompany her for all her days. Yet Hecuba warns her, "You must forget Hector, your tears cannot save him now…honor your present master and charm him with your sweet ways…and so you might raise Astyanax, the son of my son, to be the savior of Troy…and one day rebuilt it." [L 700]. But the Greeks in the last act of utmost cruelty decide to sacrifice six-year-old Astyanax. Talthybius the messenger stands tall in front of the two women. "He must be thrown from the towers…Accept it…You are powerless…You are a slave and you cannot fight alone against us…Do not call down any curses on the ships that await you…If you say anything that will anger the Greek army, they will neither allow your child's body to be buried nor lamented. Be still and accept what you cannot change, your child will be buried and you will find kindness." [L 735].

Andromache's farewell to her child is one of the most emotional glimpses into a mother's heart: "Oh darling boy, child that I prized too much…You must leave your mother, and your enemies will kill you…Oh my child, you are crying…Do you know what terrible things will happen to you? You cling to me and hide in my clothes…You are a little bird, nestling under his mother's wings…but you will fall a horrible fall…Oh dearest young thing, nestling against your mother, how sweet is your breath…Now for the last time kiss your mother; put your arms around me and kiss me…Oh you Greeks, you have found torture worse than any barbarian's…Why do you kill this child who has never done you wrong?" [L 735]

She turns to Talthybius and hands him her child. "…Take him away, throw him down…I am destroyed by the gods and cannot save my child from death." [L 740] Submissive, she climbs the wagon of war spoils that will take her to the ships.

In the end, when the little boy is killed and Andromache gone, Talthybius brings the broken body of the child into Hecuba's arms. She talks to him like if he was still alive. "...Oh my poor little child. Oh sweet mouth that made such grand promises. Grandmother, when you die I will come to visit your grave and cut off some of my curls and leave them as an offering and tell how much I love you. Dear child, you did not bury me, but I, an old woman now without a city, must bury your young corpse. Oh terrible, those kisses, and all my care for you, watching over you as you slept, all for nothing." [L 1180]

Faltering, she places the dead child on Hector's shield. Astyanax is buried. Troy is set on fire to be no more. Hecuba attempts to jump and immolate herself, but Talthybius stops her. The trumpet sounds. It is the sign for the women to start for their ships. Denied of everything, even death, they march to their life of slavery. The Chorus chant "Farewell, Farewell!...Come, you and I...Forth to the long ships, and the sea's foaming."

Women of this century, we can hold hands with Hecuba and Andromache. We are still victims of war and suffer for our children just as they did. Their words are our words. Such is the greatness of Euripides, his insight into the human heart and the plight of humanity makes him universal and everlasting.

Adriana Husta

Don't compromise yourself.
You are all you've got.
~Janis Joplin

Espana Bull

Bright lights gouge my eyes
My cathartic legs apart
I hold on to the white bull
As the crowd covers us with
Red tears while the cart rattles
Inviting the towns children behind us
Shouting, "Ava Maria."
The white bull pulls me higher
To God's Grace.

Elizabeth Lane-Stevens

You can't test courage cautiously.
~Anne Dillard

Gator
Danielle Ackley-McPhail

Baetilic

Chimneys support the Venetian sky.
In Rome, light streams through the
dome's round opening to copy itself as
a ceiling sun. Clouds enter the caves of
Orvieto through barred windows where
only doves escape. At mid-mountain, ghosts
of mules circle an ancient olive press. A well
there is so deep that no oxygen breathes at
the bottom, yet footholds in the body-size
shaft attest to human descent. Far away in
the caves of Chile, the same size shaft carries
encapsulated miners back to the sun. How can
we grasp this connection of heaven and earth?

Patricia Jakovich VanAmburg

Dragon
Wendy Hellier Stevens

*There are no rules.
That is how art is born,
how breakthroughs happen.
Go against the rules
or ignore the rules.
That is what invention is about.
~Helen Frankenthaler*

Ancient Moon

You—
golden and glorious,
haloed in a charcoal sky—
balance precariously
on clouds.
Your arrogance charming
as you sing
to us the primeval lullaby
we know as the pulsing rhythm
of our beating heart.

Below you, planes
full of travelers,
weary and listless
as your drumming,
leave an exhausted underscore
burnt into the icy air.
You beam at your own importance
and hoist yourself up
by a thread
to rest like a jewel
in Ariadne's crown.

Katie Hartlove

G

The Moon's Geography

The moon wound and wound
around like white thread
finding its place on a spool.

And then into the gauzy
clouds moon scrambled,
a white spider pinching
its spindly way across the landscape
of white chrysanthemum,
of white lotus in sky ponds.

All I had to do was rest within my eyes,
allow the lunar tug, the flowering,
the harvesting, everything
that mapless leads to home.

Rosemary V. Klein

Pyrrhic Victory

Phoenix fire fills the sky.
Clouds of sulfur rain ash down.
Melted megatons of volcanic obsidian,
bend and twist back towards the heavens.
Lightning splits and forks, electric claws
of fire phoenix reaching down, to jolt
the surface of the world alive.
Searing hot and sun-baked rocks,
feathered over by floating ash,
lie below heaven's eye,
a baleful blast of radiation,
glaring at the celestial interloper.
Wings of fire sacrifice and burn,
shielding other water worlds, from heat
and death by light.

Pam Glindeman

Moon Walking

many years ago
upon moon's cratered terrain
Neil Armstrong stepped down

then, footprints on moon
one boot after another
again and again

now, no astronauts
trespass on lunar surface—
not in our lifetime

Vonnie Winslow Crist

Epitaph
Inspired by the short story
Ringflow *by Tom Dupree*

In the aft compartment,
I alone float among the debris.
Our fragile hull, shattered by decompression.

The dead and I drift beyond Saturn's rings.
Alone,
I propel us in, to scratch our names in her dust.

Our eddy will ripple,
show Earth our final destination.
Our adventure, this manned mission, doomed

to orbit the ringed planet, just another bit
of flotsam tumbling amid her ice and rock.

A.C. Leming

G

Downing Tools

Come Liber, come Libera,
let's put down these sickles,
throw down our heavy sheaves
and quietly take our leave.
Men now have techniques of science,
their splicing and their quickening,
such cunning and such *clevering*.
They taunt the tides and atmosphere
with hot consumptive energy;
Icarus on steroids, burning every day.
Let's leave now and venture up
to that little planet with my name,
let them increase the land's fertility
without old friends close to hand.
Liberated from outmoded Goddesses,
they can strive and plan and scheme.
We'll watch from up among
the wheat grains of the asteroids
that seed heaven's blackest soil,
tempting them to follow, and to taste.
Love, it seems, is not enough,
so let them rediscover discipline.
Come Liber, come Libera,
we'll meet men again some day.

P.S. Cottier

---

*My imagination can picture
no fairer happiness than to
continue living for art.
~Clara Schumann*

---

*The creative process
is a process of surrender,
not control.
~Julia Cameron*

---

*Art is when you hear a knocking
from your soul—
and you answer.
~Terri Guillemets*

Satellite Telepathy

Farthest friend
communing by mind waves,
not words, not letters,
but hearsay and guesses.

Tattles of this or that
from daughters observing
your planet wars,
reporting via the stars.

Tidbits
tell your tales of woe,
tell me to let go;
I can't, you know.

I, in one constellation,
you in another:
ex-husband,
ex-lover.

Carolyn Cecil

G

A Stitch in Space and Time

If I were not this body,
had no mass, no chassis,
substance, bone, or skin,
I would not be tethered
to time or germ or seed,
pinched in this earthy coat,
exiled from sea-brine,
my senses jailed,
stifled in flesh and air.

Had I choice, I would
give up this meat, shun
the confines of temporal
worlds, free to be

a plume of star wrack,
a breath bodying forth
in time and dimensions,
buzz of nebulae, each pulse
a caul, an ever-expanding veil.

 Riding eddy and wrinkle
shaken from the selvage
of a fabric woven
by galactic winds, I am
rapt between layers
of a cosmic patchwork,
a single stitch marrying
those who cast a shadow
on the great loom of the void.

Patricia Budd

Rain God
Mary A. Stevens